The Shape of Veronica

Veronica's Life, Volume 1

Stephanie Bull

Published by Tau Press Ltd, 2017.

For the White Rabbit

The Shape of Veronica by Stephanie Bull.
Copyright © 2017 Tau Press Ltd. All rights reserved.
ISBN e-book: 978-1-910342-77-0
ISBN paperback: 978-1-910342-78-7
ISBN hardback: 978-1-910342-79-4

Published by Tau Press Ltd.
Edited by Zoë Markham (markhamcorrect.com).
Continuity editing by Adriel Wiggins (adrielwiggins.com).
Cover by Jane Dixon-Smith (jdsmith-design.com).

i

The eighteenth birthday of Veronica Clifford-Hughes, a beautiful and sunny midsummer's day in 1910, was not the bright social event it might have been. But then she had never celebrated a birthday the way she understood that other children of her quality and breeding did. There were never any guests and certainly no party games. Often there was not even cake.

As she lay in her bed, on her right side with her legs bent and her right arm stretched out behind—because that relieved the pressure on her back and was most comfortable—she wondered if there might be cake. It was a special day, after all, and it was the least they could do. But she was not even sure whether the staff in the house knew it was her birthday.

No, instead of parties and the whirl of Society she was imprisoned in Versyns Hall, her parents' home, on the Downs to the south-east of London, halfway to the coast. Just as she had been for all her eighteen years. Hidden from the view of decent people who would be terrified and disgusted at the sight of her. And if there was one thing she'd learnt in all those years: nobody wanted to see her.

She barely even saw the rest of the staff save for her maid, Polly, and her tutor, Mr Plumley. Sometimes she would receive a summons from the steward, Mr Laughton, particularly if she had done something deemed to be wrong. And she went to church on Sunday mornings accompanied by the ill-tempered housekeeper, Mrs Jenkins.

Veronica sometimes wondered if the people in the flying vessels that occasionally went over might look down and panic at the sight of her. But at the astonishing speeds they travelled she doubted they had even a moment to see her before landing in London, heading over the English Channel in Paris, or traveling even farther.

She couldn't see the clock from where she lay so she pushed herself up. It was barely six o'clock and it would be ages before Polly came to dress her. She sighed. Another day of intense boredom loomed ahead of her. It was a miracle she did not lose her mind with the incessant tedium of it all.

The sun shone gaily through the window as Veronica climbed from the bed and wandered over to the mirror. She stared at herself. It was the same body that always stared back at her. It did not seem strange to her but she knew her bent spine and twisted limbs made her a pariah.

She was an ugly monster. A crime against perfection. Only the lower orders were imperfect, according to Mr Laughton, and he had often expressed the idea she was a cuckoo in her parents' nest. A changeling perhaps, swapped at birth by the Fae. It was nonsense as far as she was concerned, but then Mr Laughton was barely a hands-breadth above the lower orders himself.

Her parents had given him permission to apply discipline to keep her in check. He never did it himself but he always watched when he ordered Mrs Jenkins to perform that duty. Both were intensely God-fearing folk and, to them, her deformity was a sign of the Devil.

And there she was in all her monstrous deviltry, looking back out of the mirror at herself. The morning sun was behind her and fell on her nightdress. The shape of her body was a silhouette within its halo. So slim, yet twisted.

But if she raised her hands to her eyes in such a way to blot out the abomination of her upper body, lifting her chin so her neck ached, she did not think she was so unpretty. Plain perhaps but not a monster.

She pushed the nightdress from one awkward shoulder and then the other. It caught for a moment on her back and breasts, then with a tug she dislodged it and it fell to the ground, leaving her naked. Once again she placed her hands to block the view, this time just revealing her feet.

True, she had not seen many bare feet except in pictures and in the reproductions of classical Greek statues that filled her parents' house. But her feet were not deformed. They were quite petite and elegant. She lifted one and pointed it, then the other. Of course no one was permitted to see her feet, and it would be shocking if her matching elegant ankles were revealed, even if she were not monstrous.

She rearranged her fingers to expose more of her body. Her legs were not quite straight, and it hurt to force them into a normal arrangement, but they too matched the elegance of the female statuary.

The delta at the meeting place of her thighs was a mystery to her, all the statues had that area covered. The hair there was as dark as that on her head.

But her hips were quite satisfactory and her waist went in like that of any lady. Not that she was able to wear a corset, and for that she was grateful.

It was from there up that things went awry. She dropped her hands. In a perfect woman the shoulders would be horizontal and parallel to the floor, but hers were irregular. The left was several inches higher than the right. The arch in her spine, when seen from the front, made her look like she was crouching, as if she was embarrassed by the generous proportions of her breasts.

Her knowledge of the upper female torso was informed only by the statues. Most had cone-shaped breasts that peaked like mountains. Only a couple had more rounded ones like hers and they did not have the detail of the darkened area at the summit, so she had no idea whether hers, being a hands-breadth in width, was unusual or not.

Naked, she walked to the window. It was still early and there would be no one to see her. The sun on her skin felt warm and pleasing. She stared out across the manicured lawns and precisely calculated gardens. Beyond those were the rounded sheep-grazing hills of the South Downs themselves.

The window was closed. She had received all sorts of vague warnings about leaving windows open at night which ranged from the possibility of catching diseases to attacks from strange men. Though she wondered why any man might want to climb up to her third floor window, especially as she was so re-pugnant. Anyway, it was no longer night and she wanted to breathe fresh air.

Her distorted back made it hard for her to reach up so she fetched a chair and climbed on to it. The fact that her body was now completely exposed did not concern her. She undid the lever catch at the top of the sash window and pushed up. The window stuck and she increased the pressure. It flew upwards and slammed with a great crash into the frame above.

She teetered on the chair. A wave of fear rushed through her as there was now nothing between her and a drop to the slabs of the walkway beneath. She grabbed the curtain to steady herself and relief flushed the tension from her.

Cool air rushed in and brushed across her body. The points of her breasts went hard as they sometimes did. Then she froze at the sound of someone clear-ing their throat.

Outside.

One of the gardeners stood there. He was gripping the handles of his wheelbarrow loaded with gardening implements. And he was looking up to her window.

The sun was full on her, delineating every curve of her hideously misshapen body.

'Mornin', miss,' he said in quite an ordinary voice that carried up to her through the still, cool air. She did not move.

He nodded once then looked away, lifting his barrow and heading across the gravel into the gardens.

Veronica blinked. *I should probably get down,* she thought, still following his departure. He didn't glance back. *I must be terribly ugly that he doesn't want to look.*

She shook her head and focused on climbing down. After she put the chair back, she returned to the mirror. She recalled the expression on his face. It had not been one of horror, nor even disgust. If she was not mistaken he'd had a slight smile. *Also,* she thought, *he was quite handsome.*

For a commoner.

ii

Every one of her garments, even her shoes, was specially tailored to fit her warped form. The fittings were always unpleasant affairs, the dressmakers often huffing and making faces. They also took liberties with her person, touching and prodding, as if she were nothing more than a mannequin.

But she was used to it. There had been a time, when she was young, her parents had engaged physicians, and charlatans, from across the world in an effort to repair her deformity. It was the worst time of her life. Every treatment caused excruciating pain as they tried to straighten her out.

They had all failed but it left her with a desire to be left alone since human contact was always painful. The efforts to change her had ceased at age eleven. Her monthlies had begun, her breasts and the hair between her legs had sprouted.

That was also the time when her parents had ceased to speak with her except on rare occasions they were at the house. Months might pass during which she would not see either of them. They did not write and she only saw an occasional word of them in the newspaper.

Her personal maid, Polly, was the one person she saw every day. Polly, who saw all of Veronica's body—monstrous or not.

By the time Polly came to help her dress that morning of her eighteenth birthday, Veronica had slipped back into her nightdress and returned to her bed. She was reading *The Tennant of Wildfell Hall* again. She had just read the passage where the heroine, Helen, slams the door on her debauched husband preventing him from doing ... something. The scene always made Veronica tremble with excitement—or fear, she was not sure which—because it was such a daring thing to defy one's husband.

Not that she would ever have to slam her door on a husband, debauched or otherwise. Her marriage prospects were nil, despite her parents' wealth.

Veronica allowed Polly to dress her without interfering. But the events of the early morning still preyed on her mind. She found herself staring at Polly's bosom hidden beneath her uniform. What did her breasts look like? She assumed Polly's were smaller than her own since they did not push out a great distance. Would they be cones or globes? Perhaps overall size was the determinant.

The peaks of Veronica's breasts stiffened again as Polly's hands did their work of fitting the clothes around her. Today's dress was marigold and quite light, which was appropriate for the heat, but convention still required layers of petticoats.

Polly undid her mistress's hair until it hung in dark brown ringlets. Veronica did like the shades of her hair because when the sun caught it *just so* it shone like dark honey. And because it was so long it went some way to disguising her hump, so she might even pretend she was a real person.

The maid walked through the sunlight and her blonde hair became iridescent. Veronica was not jealous; after all, she did not have to spend the day with hers tied tight into a bun. Did Polly have someone who did it for her? It was with considerable surprise Veronica realised she had not the slightest idea.

Then she wondered at herself. Such strange thoughts to be having, after so many years with not the slightest consideration of such things. And here she was, on her eighteenth birthday exposing her naked body to a young gardener, and—

'Who does your hair, Polly?'

The maid stood stock-still, half in and half out of the sun's brilliance. 'Miss?'

'Who does your hair?' Veronica repeated. 'In the mornings. You do mine, who does yours? Do you do your own?'

Polly turned slowly. Her face, initially in shadow, was revealed like the waxing moon. 'I share me room with Ursula, miss. She does mine, an' I do hers.'

'Ursula?'

'She's a housemaid, miss.'

'Oh.'

Veronica had seen the housemaids, of course. And now she knew one of them was called Ursula—which meant 'bear' in Greek—and that she did Polly's hair in the morning. With her question answered she seemed to have exhausted the subject's conversational possibilities. Particularly since, she suspected, a question about the shape of Polly's breasts might not be acceptable even to a maid. Perhaps she could find this Ursula and ask her about the shape of Polly's bosom. Which begged the question of whether they revealed each other's bodies to one another when they dressed or undressed.

Veronica frowned. She almost felt like Lewis Carroll's Alice, though Veronica's suddenly confusing world was terribly real and not a dream at all.

When Polly had finished with her, Veronica went down to breakfast as she did every day. By ten o'clock breakfast was complete and, on a normal Wednesday, it would be time for her lessons. After which there would be luncheon. Then more lessons. Veronica could speak French, German and Italian; could read Latin; and was familiar with Ancient Greek. She was well versed in Mathematics, Science and Philosophy. It was not on her tutor's syllabus but she had also educated herself as much as she could in the arts.

She received no lessons in deportment, dance or music, since those skills would never be required of her; besides, her body was not at all suited to them. Even piano playing was difficult. She was destined to live out the entire rest of her life in solitary spinsterhood; she had no need for the social arts.

But this was no ordinary day. It was her eighteenth birthday, and there were no lessons. It was like a Sunday, even though it was Wednesday.

Veronica wandered to the library. Reading was her only pleasure. It took her out of her lonely existence to places and times she could only dream about.

She sat herself on a hard-back chair by the window where the sun came through and warmed her back. The sofas and armchairs were comfortable enough but getting out of them was always a trial. Her back ached most of the time and she tried not aggravate it. The sun's warmth eased the ache somehow. She wondered how much better it might be if the rays might be allowed to strike her skin directly. Not through a window, not through the layers of clothing she had to put up with, but with the warmth directly on her naked flesh.

That put her in mind of the garden, which made her think of the young gardener. It seemed he had not been disgusted by her body although, from the angle, he would not have been able to see her back.

The peaks of her breasts hardened again. Idly she rubbed a finger across her nipple through the material of her dress, pressing against the resisting protrusion. The sensation made her blink in astonishment. It was barely describable, like the crackle of a winter fire, somewhere between pain and the most delightful pleasure.

By way of investigation, she described circles around the tip of her breast and found, even through layers of cloth, she could control the level of delight by how close she approached the tip. She moved her hand to her other breast and received the same burst of pleasure.

She placed the book in her lap and used both hands, stroking and scratching at her bosom. It was thrilling and threatened to possess her rational mind. She forced her hands into her lap, discovering she was breathing heavily. The whole process had been quite remarkable, and the feelings it engendered were by far the best birthday present she had ever had.

She could not imagine how she had never discovered this before. Was it something that only happened when one reached eighteen? She did not think so. Perhaps the strange events of the day had conspired to bring her to this point.

But where was this point?

She knew, if she had access to her naked breasts, she would be able to explore the sensation even more thoroughly. And that was something she found she was very determined to do. It was not as if any servant in the house could dictate her actions. Although, now she thought about it, that is exactly what they did. They told her when to rise, when to eat and when to sleep. It was as if she had lived all her years as an automaton.

Well, that could change. Though on reflection, if she made strange demands, the staff would most certainly report her behaviour to her father. So she would have to be circumspect with her new awakening. However, there were places where they would not follow. And, today of all days, her time was her own.

So she returned the book to its place on the shelves and headed back to her room. Forcing herself not to run.

iii

For the very first time, she realised the door to her bedroom lacked for a lock. It had never occurred to her before because there had not been a need. Privacy simply had not been a consideration, not only because she was a cripple but because she was merely female.

She looked around for some way to bar the door, perhaps a chair against it. Not much of a barrier but it would serve to delay entry if someone tried. But that in itself could be a problem if one of the servants tried to enter. She was acutely aware from her Brontë novels, and others, that women who behaved strangely were locked up either in a wing of the house, or Bedlam.

She sighed. It was quite ridiculous how difficult satisfying a simple desire could be. Of course, she could wait through all the rest of the day until she went to bed, but she was not willing to do that. This was her birthday, after all, and the throbbing temptation of her breasts had barely diminished. She desired to explore them further; to prove the point she lifted both her hands to her bosom and squeezed each breast hard. The effect almost made her swoon as shivers danced through her body.

Oh, indeed, there was no question, she must get at them unobstructed. They demanded immediate attention.

The sun's position had changed and now its beams came in at sharp angle across her bedroom floor. The window was still wide open, as she had left it. Birdsong filtered in, along with the scents of garden flowers.

She considered: When light shone on a window and a person inside was in the shade it was impossible to see them. So if she were to stand by the window in shadow with her back to the door...

She was there almost before her thought was completed. She loosened the drawstrings at the top of her bodice with fumbling fingers.

Once the top was loose enough she pulled it down over her shoulders. It stopped at her hump. Her skin seemed to burn as if she were ill. Indeed it was a kind of fever, almost as if her body was gripped in a demented dream. For the sheer pleasure of it, she ran her fingers lightly across her neck and down. She scratched her nails across the place where her bosom swelled from her chest and bit down on a groan that attempted to emerge unbidden from her throat.

She stopped. She was breathing even more heavily, as if she had been exerting herself. It had been a long time since she had run, since that was not seemly for a lady, or indulged in any sort of physical game. There were few she could do; croquet was possible but that never left her breathless.

What was happening to her?

Then it came to her: *sins of the flesh*. Every Sunday she attended church and listened to how Jesus was good and kind, but his Father was vengeful and full of wrath. It didn't make a lot of sense to her. She was taught that men were good and strong, while women were weak and sinful. It seemed she was not permitted pleasure in this life and that the next would be a reward. However, as far as she could determine, she was already cursed and there was no place in Heaven for her.

Up to this point she had had no idea what *sins of the flesh* were but her current actions were extremely pleasurable—in a curious way—and it certainly involved flesh. So this must be what the Reverend Albert Peacock was talking about. And, if she was already cursed, she might as well enjoy it.

With that thought she dipped her right hand inside her bodice and lifted out her left breast. Warm air drifted across the skin, and it almost glowed in the light from the window. She held her breast and showed it to the world, the danger of it thrilling her. Just as she had been exposed to the gardener this morning, she presented her breast with its erect nipple, even though she knew no one could see even if they looked.

She looked down and realised she had never examined her own body in detail. In the daylight she could see small hairs scattered sparsely across the surface. The line where the dark patch began was clearly delineated, and the nipple stood out from its pimpled surface. Gently she squeezed her breast, pressing her fingers into the softness. This time she was unable to cage the groan as it fought its way from her throat.

She bit her lip and glanced guiltily around the room as if Polly or another servant might be spying on her. The room remained empty. Looking out the window she saw "her" gardener working on a flowerbed halfway down the ornamental rockeries. His shirt was stained with sweat and he had the sleeves rolled up. He knelt on one knee as he dug a trowel between the flowers. His arms were hairy and muscled, and his hair fell forward over his face as he worked.

Lust—she remembered—of the seven deadly sins, that was the one associated with the sins of the flesh. She wondered why she had never looked in the dictionary to determine its meaning. But she knew she did not need to be told what it meant any more. This feeling she had inside her, it was lust.

She squeezed her breast again. The feeling was still there but diminished. She needed to do more. She dug her nails into the flesh. The sensation redoubled. Slowly she released the pressure and glanced down. She could see the curved indentations where her nails had been. Smiling, she scraped her nails across the bare tip and shuddered. The pleasure was the most exquisite pain.

With her left hand she released her right breast from its confinement and repeated the process, first with one hand and then both. She grabbed each nipple and pulled. She had almost ceased rational thought. Every facet of her attention was focused on her breasts, and the only thing she desired was more of the same.

She rubbed across them with the palms of her hands, relishing the way her now bullet-hard nipples were bent and dragged. She was hot and panting though she no longer cared. Even if Polly had walked in on her, she did not think she would stop now. She grasped her left breast in both hands and squeezed hard. The end bulged and her nipple stood out. She twisted her hands so her breast tilted upwards. She stared in fascination at the dark flesh pointing directly at her. She opened her mouth and pulled the end closer. Her neck and back ached as she stretched downward.

Her tongue flicked out and lapped. She shivered and moaned. Ignoring the pain as her back stretched, she engulfed the nipple with her mouth and sealed it inside. She sucked hard then ran her tongue around and along it. Her breast muffled her own squeal of ecstasy.

Something was happening inside.

It was as if she had become a keg of powder with a lit fuse. She could not have extinguished the fire even if she desired to do so—and that thought was the absolute furthest thing from her mind.

The suction of her mouth held the breast in place as she transferred her right hand to her other, and kneaded it like bread dough. The pressure inside her grew, like a steam boiler with too much heat, she felt as if she going to explode and nothing could stop her. Her face creased in delightful agony as the feelings inside tried to escape. She only had to open the door. If she only dared.

Her whole being erupted in pain and ecstasy. She cried out, releasing her captive breast from her mouth. She pressed each breast hard against her chest as waves of pleasure shot through her.

Then, almost as fast as the feeling had come over her, it ebbed away. She stood before the window panting. She still gripped her breasts, gently squeezing them as the feelings drifted from her, like mist in the early morning sun.

She was drained of energy but content. She opened her eyes.

At first she could not focus, then the window frame resolved, followed by the outside world. There was a movement. The gardener was on his feet and looking toward the house. With a shock of guilt she realised she must have cried out and that he had heard her.

The sun still shone through the window to her side. The brightness of the Georgian stones of the building would make this window nothing more than a dark hole.

But he had heard her.

She did not move. Her hands covered her breasts. She stared down at him. There was no indication he could see her—though what difference would that make considering he had seen her entire body that morning.

She shook herself free from the mesmeric effect of the lust that had overcome her. She stood there, still half-naked and in full view of the gardener. She dropped her hands, exposing herself. Brazen. He gave no reaction, so she was sure now he could not see her.

Her heart had slowed in its pounding. Her breathing no longer came in frantic bursts. She considered how she felt. Certainly more relaxed than before, even her back had ceased to hurt. Could the sating of her lust provide respite from the aches? It seemed they might.

She knew she should feel guilty as the gently moving air wafted across her bare chest, but that was not how she felt at all. She felt a release, as if something had been building within her for many years and had, at last, had a chance to escape, albeit for a very short time.

Carefully, because she found they were now quite tender, she hid her breasts back inside her clothes and tightened the drawstrings. She took a step back into the room and as her thighs rubbed together she realised they were wet. She frowned, it had been many years since she had lost control of herself. She checked the floor where she had been standing, it was still dry so it had not been bad. Still, if the sating of lust caused her to lose control she would have to be careful. Perhaps use a cloth.

She glanced into the garden once more. The gardener was back at his work.

The outer world had barely changed.

But, to her inner world, it was as if Atlantis had emerged from beneath the waves. It was enough to compensate for the lack of cake.

iv

The next few mornings became something of a ritual. She woke when the sun's light breached the room. She would place the chair by the window and open it. Then she removed her nightdress and sat naked massaging and pinching her breasts, enjoying the gentle stimulation that flowed through her, until the gardener appeared.

Then she would climb up on the chair again as he passed.

She did not even need to attract his attention. From the very next day, he would pause and set down his barrow. With a pretence of moping his brow he looked around until his eyes came to rest on her window. He studied her body for a few moments, then touched his finger to his forelock and went about his business.

It was their secret and it was the most connected she had ever been to another human being, though they had never uttered a word to one another. It was a thing she appreciated almost more than the climactic moment she achieved shortly afterwards when she cried out to him in her ecstasy.

As the days passed, the delicious sensations did not become less, nor did they become more, but somehow broader and deeper. And her desire to achieve them became a constant in the back of her mind.

Even during her lessons with the hesitant Mr Plumley.

He was, perhaps, in his fifties and while the hair on his head had not thinned, it had become quite grey. He always had a slightly yellow quality to his skin, and eyes which she had discovered was a constant mild jaundice.

While she studied him, she was quite certain he had never done more than cast the swiftest glance at her in the five years he had been teaching her. He spoke quietly, with a slight hitch on certain words, but on the subjects he taught he also spoke with authority.

She did not dislike the fellow—though she knew he thought of her as all others did: as a twisted corruption of a woman. But he was never impolite.

It was after her discovery of lust that she looked at him with different eyes. Where before she had simply glanced, now she stared. If he was aware of it he gave no sign. She knew there was something that happened between men and women, because of the oblique exhortations to avoid it that were handed out in church.

She wanted to ask Mr Plumley but she doubted he would appreciate the question. If it was a sin to perform then it must be a bad manners, at the very least, to discuss.

There were lessons on Saturday, though they did not extend into the afternoon since Mr Plumley played cricket in the local village team. So after luncheon she was free once more.

The gardener had behaved differently that morning. When he stopped, and before he looked up at her nakedness, he had removed his shirt. Veronica had stared at his exposed chest, absorbing the many muscles delineated under his rippling skin, just like the athletic statues. But where they were cold pale stone he was bronzed by the sun and so very alive.

To have one's skin tanned that way marked one as being of the lower classes. Those of Veronica's rank did not go out in the sun except with suitable protection in the form of long sleeves and high necks, as well as a parasol. She had seen pictures. However, the revelation of his torso made her consider that perhaps being a shade of bronze just meant you were like a classical statue, and beautiful to behold.

Back in the classroom, the prospect of the long and boring afternoon persuaded her that she must, finally, change her behaviour even though it might risk comment, and even censure. But perhaps she could gain a form of permission.

'Mr Plumley?' she said quietly in the middle of conjugating Latin verbs related to ownership. He almost jumped out of his skin.

'Miss ... ah ... Clifford-Hughes?' It was as if he had trouble remembering her name. He lifted his head and looked into the distance somewhere past her left ear.

'I have learnt a great deal of botany with you, and I have found it to be most elucidating'—she paused—'however I wondered whether it might not be unreasonable to indulge in a little more practical study?'

He seemed at a loss to know what to say. It was, in fact, the most words she had spoken to him in a very long time, perhaps ever.

'That is an ... ah ... interesting p-p-proposition.'

'Thank you,' she said. 'I'm so pleased you feel the same way. It has occurred to me that, one day, I will have to occupy my own time and, it seems to me, cultivating flowers is something I may enjoy during my solitary years. Do you not think so?'

'Yes, of course, a very f-forward-thinking idea.'

Veronica smiled at him, though she knew he would never see it. She wondered whether, if she were to stimulate her bosom right now, even expose them, whether he would see that. In her heart she thought he probably would, something told her that men—gardener, tutor, or gentleman—would *always* notice that. (Otherwise why would there be a prohibition against men and women being alone together?)

Their conversation must be at an end, she thought, as he returned his attention to the volume he had been studying. In a burst of wanton daring she raised her left hand and squeezed her right breast making no attempt to disguise it.

He did not look up. Perhaps they didn't always notice.

Once Mr Plumley had departed and luncheon had been accomplished, Veronica went to her room and rang for Polly, quite against her usual habit. The maid arrived several minutes later panting somewhat, a flush in her cheeks and, if Veronica was not mistaken, a slightly glazed look, as if her attention was not fully in the present.

'You rang, miss?'

'I need to change, I am going for a walk.'

One would think the sun had fallen from the sky and landed at Polly's feet.

'A walk, miss?'

'Quite so.' Veronica knew this was precisely the sort of thing that might be reported to her parents (wherever they were) but she had prepared for it. 'Mr Plumley thinks it would be a good idea for me to take up practical botany.'

'Botany, miss?'

'The study of plants. So I wish to look around the gardens to see what plants I might like to cultivate.'

'Yes, miss.'

Veronica allowed Polly to set about the undressing and redressing process. She even found the aching in her back was barely noticeable as Polly removed her outer garments. Veronica's senses were heightened. When her maid gave her her hand, so Veronica could step out of the ring of dress material on the floor, her fingertips touched the girl's skin as if it had never touched her before. The warmth, the slight wrinkles at the joints, and how delicate they seemed.

Polly approached very close as she tightened the belt at the waist of the new dress, and a scent Veronica knew drifted from her maid. It was the same scent Veronica herself made, when she stimulated her breasts.

The mistress smiled a secret smile. The reason her maid had been delayed in arriving, the reason for being out of breath, and why she had colour in her cheeks. The same reason it happened to Veronica, every morning.

'Perhaps you should accompany me?' said Veronica. 'I may want to speak to one of the gardeners and that would be inappropriate if I were on my own.'

'Yes, miss.'

Veronica frowned a little. Did she detect a certain disappointment? Perhaps her maid wanted to go back to whatever she had been doing before. If it had been Veronica she would have as well, but that was just too bad. The maid would simply have to wait before returning to pleasuring herself.

V

I t took a few minutes for a parasol to be located. Veronica stood in the main hall and felt all the staff were staring at her. She never went out except on Sundays, or on special occasions, and taking a spin around the garden had every maid and boy who could find an excuse coming through the hall to look.

'Miss Veronica?'

The housekeeper emerged from below stairs. Mrs Jenkins was as thin as a stair-rod which only emphasised her considerable bosom. Her voice echoed through the hall and the other staff vanished as if they had never been there.

'Mrs Jenkins?' Veronica bit back an automatic apology. Instead she smiled, though she had to strain to lift her chin to ensure it was visible.

'You are going outside.'

'Mr Plumley has come up with an excellent plan,' she said. 'Something to occupy me. Horticulture.'

'Mr Plumley suggested this?'

'We discussed it.'

'I see.'

Veronica knew the woman was looking for some way to stop her but, after all, what harm could there possibly be in the raising of flowers?

Finally she said, 'I was not informed.'

'Oh, I am so sorry.'

It was at that moment Polly returned with the parasol. She hurried into the hall, noticed Mrs Jenkins and slowed to a sedated walk. Veronica did not even know whether the housekeeper was popular with the other staff. She suspected not.

'We must get approval from your parents,' said Mrs Jenkins.

'Of course,' said Veronica, her heart sinking. 'However, I am prepared for the outside now, perhaps I might look at the flowers and see if there is anything that takes my fancy? With Polly accompanying me, of course.' It was a bold ploy.

It took long seconds for Mrs Jenkins to decide that, after all, there was no harm in it, and being in the garden did not break the rules imposed by the girl's parents.

She nodded, turned and left.

Veronica breathed a sigh of relief. Polly approached and handed her the parasol.

Together they went through into the ballroom. It was not a room Veronica entered often—there were no parties or balls—but it provided the most direct access to the gardens.

One of the French doors was thrown open and Veronica stepped out into the sun. If she could she would have turned her face to the sky to drink in the rays of solar warmth—as if she herself was a bud opening its petals. But she was not physically able, forced as she was to look down most of the time, so instead she took the parasol and, with an unpractised hand, raised it awkwardly.

She wondered where "her" gardener was. She had a great desire to see him up close, to smell him and touch him. She stumbled on a crooked stone but managed to catch herself, though a pain shot through her back.

'Are you all right, miss?' said Polly, suddenly at her side.

'Yes, of course.' In her thoughts the words were followed by *I am not a cripple* but that is just what she was. A cripple and a monster, unfit to associate with other humans.

And yet. The gardener had not only become part of her secret, he had joined in. But then, a nagging part of her mind said *he cannot see the hump.*

She raised herself up as straight as she could manage, determined to see if he continued to enjoy looking at her body and revealing his, after he had faced the monster in person.

They started along a path flanked by carefully constructed beds with their tiered arrangements of living colour. Glancing this way and that, she did recognise some of the varieties but most were unknown to her. However, she did not wish to expose her ignorance just yet. And if her deception was to be complete she would have to learn about them in reality. She might even enjoy it.

Veronica did not know how many gardeners the house had but as she walked she spotted two older ones she vaguely recalled having seen from the windows. She and Polly reached the end of the path and turned right, before turning right again and heading back towards the house along the middle avenue.

The scents of summer were quite delightful and bird song filled the air. In the distance, on the slopes of the Downs, there were sheep and cattle. Over the fields, hanging motionless in the air with their wings beating so fast they were invisible, were hawks. Every now and then one would stoop on its prey. The idea of a small creature like a rabbit dying beneath the cruel talons gave her a thrill. She almost felt like that herself. As if she were a hawk, waiting to dive on her prey.

And there he was.

She forced herself not to stare. He was no closer than when he looked in her window (and when he heard her cry out from pleasure) but now she was on the same level as him. The separation of three floors when she exposed herself was both a defence and a barrier. She was a princess in a high tower and he was ... not her prince; he was still just the gardener.

But now she was not safe in her tower and, even though she was fully clothed, she felt exposed in a different way.

It was the task of servants to work without being visible, so when she and Polly approached, he melted away like ice under the summer sun. Still, she hoped he understood she was looking for him. She dared not search him out, and kept her eyes on the beds.

With Polly trailing behind, she moved forward with slow, controlled steps and finally reached the place where he had stood. One of his small spades was stuck into the earth, its smooth wooden handle protruding towards her. It might have been her imagination, must have been since she had never been close enough to catch his scent, but she believed she could smell his earthiness in the still, hot air.

She stared down at a group of flowers with yellow and blue petals. 'I do not know this plant,' she said, turning to Polly and speaking in a loud voice. There was a movement in the corner of her eye but she forced herself not to turn towards it. 'Do you think, Polly, we could find someone?'

''Scuse me, ma'am,' said her delicious man from almost behind her. His almost growling voice sent a shiver through her, and made her breasts tingle with its vibration.

She turned abruptly. 'You should not sneak up on a body, you gave me quite a shock.'

He backed off, staring down. 'Sorry, miss.'

He had his shirt on but it was tight and followed the contours of his muscles. She had often read, in the more melodramatic stories, of how women swooned when their man came close. What she felt was not a desire to swoon; on the contrary, she wanted to touch him, to leap on him. She wanted to feel his coarse and hairy chest, to count his ribs—and to discover whether the nipples on his chest reacted the same way as hers.

'Miss?' It was Polly's voice that pierced her reverie. Veronica tore her gaze away from him. It was most inappropriate. She tried to remember what she was supposed to be saying.

He saved her. 'Were it this flower you were asking for, miss?'

His grammar was appalling but she adored the earthy burr from the back of his throat that emerged with every word. It was certainly enough to forgive his lack of education. His voice dragged her back to his face.

'I...'

The world faded away and all she could see was his face. Dark hair in a tumble framing his face, brown eyes, untidy beard. He was like a rural Lord Byron. She wanted to get a pair of scissors and cut his hair back, tidy the beard, though she did not have the skill, she wanted to learn so she could do it. Her heart pounded.

'Miss?' said Polly again.

I'm talking to a man I don't know, yet who has seen me in all my nakedness.

He broke the spell by moving forwards and, without touching her, stepped up to the flowerbed and knelt down. She turned as he moved and caught his scent. Not how she imagined, it was sharp like vinegar but sweet. He was kneeling at her feet. His rough hand reached out to a plant whose flowers burst from the end of long green stalks wrapped in its even longer leaves.

'Did thee mean this, Miss Veronica?'

He turned his head, his gaze fell on the hem of her dress where her booted feet were hidden, then moved up her body. She almost gasped as his gaze passed across her midriff and to her breasts. Encased though they were in layers of cloth it felt as if he were seeing her to her skin. As well he might, he *knew* her.

It was as if they were now posed as they were every morning. Him below, with her in the window displaying her body to him. Of its own volition her right hand crept from where it rested at her waist, edging towards her left breast.

She shook herself. And her hand dropped back. 'Not that one. The yellow one in front.'

His hand shifted to brush the petals of the smaller flower.

'Yes.'

'Lover's Heart.'

vi

She could barely sleep that night in anticipation of the morning. The night was so hot she pulled back the sheets and removed her nightdress. Her skin burned; though whether it was the summer night or the thought of him she did not know.

The image of him, the sound of his voice, him saying her name *Veronica*, the smell he left in the air, it all conspired to rob her of her rest. She rolled from one side to the other, always face down.

Finally she sought release in lust. She dug her nails hard into her breasts as she moaned in desire and pain. Her passion ebbed, flowed and crashed like storm waves on a beach. In the end she fell asleep still spasmodically clutching at her breasts.

The next thing she knew was the sound of Polly coming into her hot and sticky bedroom.

She blinked in confusion before realizing *she had missed her assignation.* She was also lying naked on the bed with Polly moving about the room. She felt nothing but embarrassment. She knew it was foolish; after all, the maid often saw her naked and even knew when her monthlies were due, but to be lying in bed in this manner seemed somehow wrong.

But the deed was done and if it were truly a crime then it had already been committed. She pushed herself up and sat on the edge of the bed. Polly was collecting her church-going clothes. Veronica frowned and then remembered. Today was indeed Sunday. She sighed. There was so little to distinguish each day from the next it was easy to become confused.

She rubbed her eyes. The bad night had left its mark. She was very tired.

Then she noticed her fingers, crusted with something brown, that was also embedded beneath her nails. Using the nail of her left index finger, she scraped at the brittle stuff on her right hand. It came off readily enough but as she worked at it, Polly bustling about preparing her wash basin, Veronica saw with horror her breasts were smeared with the dried on stuff as well.

Wetting her finger she tried to rub it off before Polly noticed. Not only was there too much, she discovered her desperate passion of the night before was the cause: she had dug her nails so hard into her breasts she had broken the skin and caused herself to bleed.

Then Polly said: 'Oh.'

Veronica looked up in shock. She had been so intent she had not realised her maid had come over and was looking at her. Veronica looked into Polly's eyes and, perhaps for the first time, the girl looked back into hers.

Veronica felt she ought to say something, to take command, but her mortification was complete. There was nothing in her mind save for total embarrassment.

Polly shifted her weight from one foot to the other. 'Let me fetch a cloth, miss.'

Her maid went across to the dresser. She dropped the face cloth into the water, then picked up the bowl and brought it to the bed. Carefully she set it down on the rug at Veronica's feet, crouched down and wrung out the cloth to remove the excess water.

Kneeling up, she took Veronica's right hand and gently wiped it. The dried blood came away easily enough and a couple of rinsings had the back of it clean of brown stains. She turned Veronica's hand over and repeated her ministrations. She checked between each finger and cleaned where needed.

Rising smoothly she went to fetch the tool for cleaning under nails and worked the dried blood out. She went through the same ritual on the other hand which Veronica watched as if she were entirely disconnected.

Polly stood up again. 'Please excuse the liberty, miss, but if you would sit sideways on the bed and let me sit beside you?'

Veronica was not entirely sure that she was not dreaming as she turned, still naked, on the bed. Polly picked up the cloth once more. Hesitantly she reached out and cupped Veronica's right breast and held it gently as she wiped the blood-encrusted skin. She ran the cloth from Veronica's shoulder down to the tip.

The effect was instant. The tips of Veronica's breasts grew and hardened. Veronica had not thought she could be more embarrassed than she had been, but now she simply wished to die and be buried.

Polly made no comment but continued to clean, though her grip became firmer. The half-moon cuts from Veronica's nails became obvious as the streaks of blood were removed. Polly paid them particular attention, ensuring they were clean, but they had closed up and were not bleeding.

'Excuse me,' said Polly quietly as she released Veronica's breast but then took a firmer hold of the dark summit between her thumb and fingers. She lifted it so she could clean underneath. The familiar warmth of lust materialised in Veronica's body, and there was nothing she could do to restrain it. And nothing to hide it as the heat of a flush emerged around her neck and in her cheeks.

Polly gently transferred her ministrations from one side to the other. Veronica gripped the side of the bed with her fist and tried to will herself to calm. It was hopeless, not only that but she could feel the wetness forming between her legs and she knew, when she finally stood, there would be a damp patch.

She shivered as the cloth stroked her breast and Polly's hand held it firmly. Then her maid squeezed and released, squeezed and released. Veronica, who had been staring blankly at the wall, looked straight at her maid in astonishment. *What was she doing?* The feelings of lust redoubled and Veronica's breathing became faster.

Polly finished wiping the top of the breast and adjusted her grip. This time she grasped Veronica's breast by the nipple alone and lifted, giving it a twist as she did so. Veronica choked back a moan and closed her eyes. She had trouble believing her maid was doing this to her but was powerless to stop it—not even sure she wanted to. The cold damp cloth stroked the underside like a poker raking hot coals, while the fingers of Polly's other hand squeezed, pulled and twisted the nipple.

'Stop,' Veronica groaned as the velvet explosion coursed through her. She shuddered and did not know how she remained sitting as her muscles convulsed and then went limp. The hands that had given her pleasure left her. She heard the swish of Polly's skirts as she picked up the bowl, and then the sound of the water being thrown away.

THERE WAS NO BREAKFAST before church. Instead Veronica was dressed in plain, restraining, demure clothes and led down to the entrance hall where Mrs Jenkins awaited, similarly attired.

A grey bonnet was added to the ensemble and they set out into the growing heat of the day. They did not take a carriage because the church was only a mile away, following the track towards the local village.

Veronica was light-headed from her lack of sleep, the heat, and the after-effects of Polly's attentions. She really did not know what to think. That she had felt pleasure from her maid's touch was without question, she had even reached the summit of that pleasure just as easily as when she had attended to herself. Not only that, but Polly had intended it. Why?

'Kindly do not dawdle, Miss Veronica,' said Mrs Jenkins. 'We do not wish to be late.'

In an effort not to attract any further attention, Veronica pushed the thoughts of the morning away and struck out at a faster pace with her walking stick. The stick eased the strain on her back a little by transferring the pressure above her hump, she supposed that two sticks might be even better but she hated appearing like an old woman.

Belonging to one of the more well-off families in the area Veronica should have been sitting in the expensive pews, with a cushion. But she was not allowed because of her deformity. As if it were an insult to the Almighty. Instead their accustomed place was at the back and to the left, on the end. As far as possible from everyone else and further back than even the lowest families.

The interior of the church was cool at least.

vii

The service lasted an hour and a half. The sermon still rang in her ears as the Reverend Peacock had, once again, flayed his congregation over their lustful thoughts and associated sins. Now the words had more meaning for her, she listened more closely, but they did not communicate much more than they ever had: Acts of lust were sinful, and that was that. All she could glean from his words was that there was more than one act of lust available, and they usually involved a man and a woman.

The idea of acts of lust with men interested her—her attraction to the gardener was a testament to that—but she still could not imagine what they might be. Was the touching of her own breasts sinful? Was it sinful what Polly had done?

The memory of it made her hot once more. She was fairly sure the sins of the flesh were not limited only to man and woman. Her thighs became slippery and she shifted her position. The wooden pews were not comfortable for someone with a normal body shape, while for Veronica they inflicted torture after no more than half an hour.

Yet she was so tired, the church so warm, and the memories of Polly's delicious touch so relaxing that, more than once she found herself drifting off. Even when forced to her knees for prayers.

On one occasion Mrs Jenkins jabbed her in the side with her elbow to bring her back to the present.

Infuriating rivulets of sweat inched down her back. Veronica pressed her spine against the back of the pew but it did no good: her hump got in the way. She growled mentally. Then more drops formed around her neck and ran down between her breasts. They itched terribly and she desperately wanted to scratch them. But she had to grit her teeth and put up with it instead.

Finally it was over. Reverend Albert Peacock gave a final blessing and processed down the central aisle, flanked by the choir boys. The congregation sang the last hymn *Lord! May the inward grace abound*, and that was the end of that for the week since she was not required to attend Evensong as well.

Veronica and Mrs Jenkins remained seated while the rest of the village and manor folk got up and made their way out. As usual there were the surreptitious glances in her direction. She pretended not to notice, finding it easier to simply keep her head down as if she was still praying—perhaps for a divine intervention that might straighten her back, thus making her invisible and unnoticed.

At least that was how she had behaved every week that she had attended the Sunday service in all the years she had been alive. While she had borne the embarrassment of being paraded before the general population. But she had changed. Now she glanced up to look at the people as they followed the vicar from the church. She saw Polly, in her Sunday Best, walking beside a tall red-haired girl whose face was a mass of freckles with barely a space for normal skin.

Polly glanced towards Veronica, looked away almost immediately—though not before meeting her mistress's eye—and then put her arm through her companion's. Was it a sign to indicate that this was Ursula?

The congregation filed out slowly and steadily. Behind the servants came the more well-to-do families, such as the Millers with their gaggle of seven children of all ages. Even Mr Nesmith, a portly but energetic man in his fifties who, as Veronica understood it, ran a law firm in the city. He had come to the house sometimes when her father was there.

She had never spoken to any of these people. She had never been introduced. She was nothing more than a shadow of sin, who lived up at the big house. A thought crossed her mind, one she had never had before.

It's not fair.

She glanced up at the stained-glass window at the end of the nave behind the altar with the big brass crucifix. The image pictured the young girl, St Agnes, with a lamb at her side and halo above her head, about to be slaughtered by a Roman soldier.

Veronica had long since looked up the history of St Agnes but failed to find out much beyond her being a martyr at the age of thirteen. Still she did know that Agnes was the patron of young girls, and gardeners. Veronica allowed herself a slight smile as she thought of *her* gardener.

The departing people had thinned out and Mrs Jenkins was making moves in readiness for them to leave. They must wait until everyone else had gone so that she did not scare anyone.

Finally the church was empty. Mrs Jenkins rose from her seat while Veronica, gripping the back of the pew in front for support, got to her feet. Her back ached terribly. The two of them, Mrs Jenkins in the lead, walked along the back of the church.

Sunlight streamed through the door like a raging fire. Veronica squinted against the light. Someone who she could only see in silhouette stood in the arch beyond, still talking to the vicar. Mrs Jenkins stopped so abruptly Veronica nearly walked into her. They waited. More drops of sweat formed and rolled across Veronica's skin beneath her clothes.

There was an arrangement of flowers near the door, as there was almost every week and even in winter there was something. Veronica recalled hearing the vicar's wife, before she died in childbirth, had a particular fondness for flowers and the vicar always ensured there was an arrangement in her honour. Two thoughts struck her at the same time, on the one hand how sad it must be to lose one's lifelong spouse (and new child in this instance), the other being that she might be able to use this to her advantage.

The enormity of what she was considering astounded her. She had certainly read many stories where someone connived to achieve their aims, but to actually do it? Was it possible or was it merely something that occurred in stories? But then she already had. Should she do more? Would she not be damned for it? She gave a little shrug; she was already damned so what difference would it make?

Mr Nesmith, for that was who it was, finally shook hands with the vicar, put on his hat, and moved away.

Mrs Jenkins waited a few moments and then stepped into the blazing sunlight. The vicar himself, wisely, had placed himself in the shade of the arch, although the movement of the sun threatened to encroach on him very soon. The choirboys had been dismissed and were playing some sort of chase game around the yew tree at the edge of the graveyard.

"An enlightening sermon, vicar," said Mrs Jenkins.

"That's very kind of you, Mrs Jenkins," said the vicar.

There was an awkward pause. The housekeeper turned to look at Veronica. This was the point where she was also supposed to thank the vicar.

"Yes, thank you, vicar."

Tradition and manners satisfied, Mrs Jenkins bade goodbye to him. The last of the rest of the congregation was gone. The working classes across to The Roman pub just opposite, and the middle classes to their shops and houses to spend the rest of the day in contemplation.

Veronica hesitated, then: "I do like your flowers, vicar. It is a very beautiful arrangement."

Mrs Jenkins came to a sudden halt and turned slowly. Veronica kept her eyes to the ground, which was the easiest for her anyway. She could not distinguish the waves of embarrassment from the heat of the sun.

"It is most kind of you to say so, Miss Clifford-Hughes." He stopped, his voice was almost a croak when he repeated: "Most kind."

Veronica half-turned towards him, though she could only see the hem of his cassock brushing the dusty stonework. "My tutor has suggested I take an interest in horticulture."

Mrs Jenkins made a noise in her throat though it was difficult to interpret. Veronica guessed she had now broken a hundred rules, the very least of which was speaking out of turn to a man, and worse, that man was the vicar.

But then what possible rules could she have broken? They had been speaking to him anyway, as they did every week.

"Well, that is most interesting, Miss Clifford-Hughes, and do you have a plan?"

"I confess, sir, I do not. Though I hope I may use a part of one of the greenhouses at the hall."

"A greenhouse is indeed an excellent idea. What varieties of plant would you like to grow?"

Veronica sighed. "Sadly, sir, I am not very knowledgeable on the subject as yet but I do hope to become so." Which was when the rest of her plan coalesced in her mind. "I hope I may learn what is needful from my father's library."

There was a steam boiler ready to explode just six feet from her, and its name was Mrs Jenkins. And yet Veronica was sure she had played her game with such exquisite delicacy and deference it would be impossible for anyone to claim she had engineered the outcome.

"Books cannot teach you all that you need to know, Miss Clifford-Hughes," said the vicar, placing his hand lightly upon her arm. "I would be quite delighted to instruct you in the subject."

"Sir, you are too kind," she said. "I could not possibly distract you from your duties."

"Nonsense, I'm sure I can find an hour here or there."

"I must defer to Mrs Jenkins, sir, she must make the final decision. She has my best interests at heart."

Veronica turned a little and raised her head so she could see Mrs Jenkins despite the strain the action caused in her back. The conflict in the woman was like the Battle of Waterloo, the differing sides throwing themselves at one another.

But it was utterly impossible for Mrs Jenkins to deny him.

"That will be entirely satisfactory, of course, vicar."

The woman's lips barely moved as she spoke, and her body was rigid.

Veronica felt triumphant though not a little nervous. Until now it had been possible for Mrs Jenkins to have written to her parents in such a manner that they would not approve her indulging in horticulture, if only approved of by her tutor. But if the vicar was offering to assist her, there was nothing her erstwhile guardians could do about it.

viii

The atmosphere between her and Mrs Jenkins was icy on the return walk. Veronica was still tired but felt far more awake than she had. Mrs Jenkins now plodded where Veronica wanted to dance.

Nothing was said about the matter with the vicar.

Sunday lunch came and went. Veronica ate alone as was typical, and then spent the afternoon in the library. She found some books on horticulture and dedicated herself to them until tea time. It turned out her knowledge of Latin was, at last, a genuine benefit.

With the sun no longer on the ballroom or the patio, she took herself out into the air. Polly was sent to locate a suitable chair which was brought out by one of the menservants—a hardback chair that could provide support for her lower back with the judicious placement of cushions.

Now that her awareness of men had been awakened by the gardener, she watched the two that brought the chair. She could not observe them directly, of course, but looked in the glass of the ballroom windows as it reflected their images.

In this instance she was less impressed. Of course their bodies were completely encased in their uniforms, but even so. One of them had been seriously marked by a pox at a young age and his face was cratered as the surface of the Moon, as seen through a telescope. The other was shorter and significantly rounder.

And then she felt guilty, if not a little embarrassed. Had she not just passed judgement on those fellows based solely on their appearance? When she herself had a spine that could not straighten?

With that, and the assistance of Polly, she sat in the warm air protected from the sun by the shade of the manor. She had her Bible with her, as protection against Mrs Jenkins should she come looking. She did not open its pages but placed a finger in a random location as if she had just recently closed it.

Veronica sat for a while looking out at the flowers, watching birds, bees, and hoverflies. In the distance she could see her gardener at his work. He glanced in her direction from time to time, and stared when he thought she was looking elsewhere. On one occasion he stood and stretched in such a way as to emphasise the shape of his physique. She suppressed an urge to giggle but it reminded her of how he had removed his shirt the day before, and that evoked a very different sensation than humour.

The sky remained a perfect blue while the golden evening light washed across the Downs from behind the house at an ever-increasing angle. The shadows lengthened and finally, when the midges found her, she retired to her room.

———◉———

THE MEMORY OF THE GARDENER had stirred her lust and, when Polly undressed her for bed, Veronica wanted the maid to touch her again. She wanted to feel the girl's hands on her breasts, pulling at her nipples and perhaps, and the unexpected thought astonished her, sucking on them as she did herself. She breathed in deeply and attempted to push away the thought, but the image of Polly suckling on her burned into her mind.

However, the atmosphere between them was too awkward. Once more they were just mistress and servant, and the barrier was like an insurmountable wall. What she needed, as in the tale of "Pyramus and Thisbe", was a chink in the wall through which she could speak to her lover.

Lover? No one in the stories she read had a lover of the same sex. Always it was male to female, just as in all the animal kingdom—as ordained in the Bible by God himself. Except that was always for the purpose of procreation, which was a thing the Reverend Peacock touched on from time to time.

Now that she thought of it he also mentioned Greeks, and not usually in a good light. Did the Greeks take lovers of the same sex? They hadn't been Christians. She must make a note and look into it.

But now, here she sat, naked on a chair while Polly bustled around while all Veronica desired was the girl to bring her once more to the pinnacle of physical delight.

"I saw you in church this morning."

Polly was turning down of the bed. "Yes, miss."

"You were with a red-haired girl?"

"Yes, miss," said Polly picked up the dress and petticoats. She really wasn't making this any easier. Was she being deliberately obtuse?

"I thought she might be Ursula."

"Yes, miss, that's Ursula."

And then the words just tumbled out of Veronica: "Do you see her without clothes, as you see me now?"

At that moment Polly had been going into the closet to hang the dress. She paused in the doorway as if someone had taken her by the shoulder, then she pushed on into the closet.

Veronica could see her shadow moving about and worried.

Had she said gone too far? Was it possible she had only imagined what had happened that morning? Dreamed it? But she had not dreamed the blood, and even now the arcs of healing skin were visible. Veronica brought her hand up and gently squeezed her left breast, letting the energy it generated flow through her, simultaneously relaxing and invigorating.

Polly returned. Veronica went to pull her hand away and hide what she was doing but she was gripped by wantonness—yes, now she understood the word—and maintained her grasp. Polly's eyes flicked to Veronica's chest, so she gave her breast a vicious squeeze and breathed in involuntarily.

"Do you see her without clothes the way you see me?"

Polly glanced at the window—still wide and open but night was falling—then at the door.

"Nothing can be done about the door, Polly."

"I could get into trouble, miss."

"I will never betray you, Polly," said Veronica. "I don't owe them anything."

Polly shook her head. "I could be sent away without references."

"But this morning..." Veronica knew she sounded like a wilful, whining child—enough of them were brought to church. She had been massaging her breast all this time; the lust was filling her up like a bucket under a pump, and threatened to overflow.

She stood and, without hiding her body, padded across the carpet and rugs to where her maid seemed frozen to the spot.

"I need you to touch me again," she said. "I'm begging you." And with that she went down on her knees, putting her arms around Polly's waist. She held her tight, smelling the starch in her pinny and the sweat from her body.

Polly's hand touched Veronica's head. Stroked her hair.

"I'll come by earlier, miss."

ix

Veronica woke early on Monday morning. She felt refreshed after the tiredness of the previous day. She divested herself of her nightgown, climbed on the chair and opened the window wide. The air was cool with a slight wind, as if the weather might be on the verge of changing. She allowed the coolness of the breeze to wash over her as she sat by the window, and waited for her gardener. She played with her breasts idly and enjoyed the gentle feelings of pleasure that ran through her.

From the outside came the sound of someone whistling an unrecognisable tune. With a burst of excitement and anticipation, she climbed up on the chair and peered out. In addition to his, rather tuneless, whistle she heard the crunch of his boots, and the grinding of the wheelbarrow across the gravel.

There was something different this morning, something inside her, a sense of joy and she felt ... wanton. On each of the previous days, she had stood still at the window, like the nude statues that adorned the house.

That was daring in itself but today she wanted to feel herself, and pretend it was him, while he watched. Perhaps she might reach the peak of perfection as his eyes devoured her—the mere thought of it had her gasping with lust and desire.

She still had to steady herself with her right hand but she brought her left one up to her breasts. She proceeded to squeeze and pull first one then the other. The ache in her back faded as the heat of lust overwhelmed her. A low groan escaped her lips, her breathing quickened, and she closed her eyes.

The footsteps stopped and she opened her eyes. There he was, staring up at her. If she had not been so deep in desire she would have laughed at the look on his face: mouth open like a carp gulping air in a pond. Without unbuttoning it, he fair ripped off his shirt.

His dark skin shone, she could see his chest where his nipples stood as proud as hers. If only she could touch them, squeeze them, pull them, *bite them.* Then he did something strange: he put his hand between his legs.

But she had no time to ponder it, more quickly than it had ever come on her before she reached the high point of her desire and screamed out loud. So loud.

The door behind her slammed open but she was too far gone to care. Her legs were buckling beneath her and she swayed. Her grip came loose from the wall and the tides of pleasure turned to terror as the chair slid from under her.

She flung up her arm as the carpet came at her face. The impact knocked the wind out of her, and she heard the chair clattering to the floor.

"Miss!"

Polly was at her side. Splintering pains shot through her spine and she groaned.

"Are you all right?"

Veronica made a little noise that did not sound like a word.

"Shall I fetch someone?"

Panic. "No." That came out and sounded right. "No. Help me sit up."

Polly held her hand as she pushed herself up and sat back on the floor, the roughness of the woven carpet digging into her bare behind.

"Oh, miss, your nose."

"What—" Veronica saw a bright spot of red on the carpet where her head had been. "Oh."

At that moment there was a scrabbling at the window and a hand shot over the windowsill. Another one followed then the concerned brown face of the gardener. He looked in with as much surprise as they did looking at him.

"Is thee orright, Miss Veronica? I saw thee fall."

Polly jumped up and stood in front of her mistress. "Get out, Seth, you can't be in here."

Veronica could feel the blood filling her nasal passageways and trying to clog up her throat, she swallowed. "No, let him in."

"But, miss," said Polly emphatically, "you have no clothes on."

"He's seen it before."

That comment stole all the winds of affront from Polly's sails. She opened and closed her mouth once or twice, saying nothing as the blood dripping from Veronica's nose, then went off to fetch a damp flannel from the basin. Seth pushed himself higher and rolled into the room, his boots landing noisily on the polished floorboards.

"You'll have the whole house on us," said Polly. "You'll be imprisoned, I'll be out on my ear, and the mistress will be locked away forever."

"I'll go if thee wants, Miss Veronica."

She raised her head a little, partly to let Polly clean her and also so she could see Seth's face. He had remained sitting against the wall below the window. He had not paused to put his shirt back on when he saw her fall, so there he was. His chest bare, his bones and muscles an undulating terrain of bronzed flesh. He had a scattering of dark hair that emphasised the valley between the hilltops where his nipples stood erect.

For his part, as she finally managed to raise her eyes above his exquisitely rounded shoulders, he was as much fixated on her breasts as she was on his chest. Except when his gaze dropped to the dark hair between her legs.

But her nose throbbed and Polly tutted.

"We can't do this here, miss." She stood up and turned to the under-gardener. "You. Do something useful—" she hesitated and glanced at Veronica then back "—pick the mistress up and bring her to the bed."

She said something else under her breath that Veronica only vaguely caught but sounded something like *No references*.

The task Polly had set him put a huge grin on Seth's face. Veronica was immediately unsure. Perhaps Polly was doing this to punish her, forcing her to accept the touch of the gardener before she was ready. Well, she was ready, and she yearned for his rough and dirty skin to touch hers.

Seth came over and crouched by her side. He was so close she could smell the scent of carbolic soap on his skin, and a hint of the sweat he had generated climbing the side of the house to rescue her. Like a prince in a fairy tale.

"I be putting an arm under your legs, miss, and one at your back."

She looked into his eyes, barely inches from hers, and she was suddenly embarrassed and self-conscious. Her hump. Not once had she seen his eyes stray to the contortion of her spine that had blighted her life, but if he put any pressure on it the pain would be terrible.

"What is it, miss?"

Her face must have betrayed her concern. "My back," she said. "My ... deformity."

He nodded. "Does it hurt, Miss Veronica?"

It was her turn to nod and she turned her head away.

"I'll take good care of thee, ne'er you worry."

A spot of blood dripped from the tip of her nose where it had collected and landed on her left breast, nearest him. Then his left arm slipped beneath her bare legs and his hand took a firm grip of her thigh. She breathed in sharply.

"Orright?"

She nodded, not trusting herself to speak in case it was a moan that emerged instead of words. His touch sent electrical sparks flashing through her. So much better than when she touched herself—more like Polly.

Then his hand touched her back, near the middle. Now it was as if she was connected to one of those galvanic devices used to treat all manner of ills: between his hands she felt as if her nerves were on fire. The hand at her back slid around her body until it reached the rise in her breast on the other side. She felt the desire welling up within her but it just made her nose throb all the more.

In a smooth motion he stood up, lifting her as if she weighed nothing at all. It strained her back a little. He pulled her into his chest and she was forced against him. Her lower body against his stomach—she could feel his buckle pressing against her bare hip. The side of her chest against his. Her breast squashed to his, she could feel his nipple pressing into her.

The effect made her dizzy. She nestled her head into his shoulder, her lips touched his skin. She wanted to taste him but the journey lasted no time at all. In a moment they were by the bed, but her head was facing the foot.

"Come round this side, you great lummox," said Polly in annoyance.

Her view of the room swung and she caught a glimpse of Polly on the other side of the bed and Seth headed that way.

I am naked, being carried by a semi-naked man.

This sort of thing never happened in the stories she read. But it was infinitely more exciting, or would have been save for the throbbing and the ache.

Seth stood near the foot of the bed while Polly fussed with pillows. "You need to have your head back, miss. I know that's hard with your condition but we'll have to see what can be done."

She was looking away. Feeling like a naughty child, Veronica took that moment to turn her head and plant a light kiss on Seth's neck, and as she pulled away she let the tip of her tongue rake across him. If he had ever been in any doubt as to her intentions before, this would make her desires quite clear. Or would, if she understood her intentions herself. All she knew was that she wanted to touch his bare skin and have him touch hers.

Or Polly. Either would do. Both.

"There," said Polly. "Place her down, neck there."

Veronica concluded that Seth must be exceptionally strong. He laid her on the bed slowly and gently. The pillows Polly had placed supported her lower back, leaving a space for her hump and then held her neck allowing her head to drop backwards a little. It was a strain but did help.

He withdrew his arm from her back and then the other from her legs. She felt his thumb graze her behind as he retrieved his hand. It made her tingle as it scraped across her right buttock, then it touched in the place between her legs. It was like an explosion but lasted only a fraction of a second before it has scratching over the rest of her.

"You need to leave before someone sees your barrow," said Polly.

"Aye." He touched his forelock. "Si'thee anon, Miss Veronica."

She heard, rather than saw, his boots scrape on the sill as he climbed out.

"Oh just a thing, miss, if thee don't take offence at my askin'?"

"What?" said Polly, presuming to speak for her mistress.

"Why's thee not got a Faraday under tha' bed?"

"Stop talking gibberish, and leave the mistress be!"

Polly refused to caress her mistress that morning and told her, in no uncertain terms, that she must stop behaving so recklessly.

Veronica bore her maid's remonstrations, but was far more curious about Seth's passing remark than being chastised. She knew what a Faraday was.

X

Polly had done all she could for her mistress's damaged nose but it could not be hidden since, even with ice fetched from the store, the swelling did not reduce greatly and there was obvious bruising.

Mrs Jenkins had to be informed.

Veronica and Polly concocted the story that Veronica had tripped awkwardly on the corner of a rug and gone over. It was not too far from the truth and not unreasonable since falling over the turned-up corner of a rug or carpet was a common-enough occurrence.

Polly received a reprimand for allowing it to happen, while it was strongly implied this was God's punishment for Veronica being so forward with the vicar. Veronica was instructed to remain in her room for at least the rest of the day if not the following one. A command that suited Veronica, and she requested (with suitable humility) that Polly stay with her to fetch anything needed.

Mrs Jenkins seemed to think this too was some sort of punishment. Polly was in a curious position within the household since she was just a housemaid who had been assigned to provide for Veronica, functioning more as a lady's maid, which normally had considerably higher status (and pay). If Veronica had been the lady of the house, Polly would have been second only to Mrs Jenkins herself, and certainly not under her control.

But officially she remained a housemaid with specific duties to Veronica which meant, much of the time, she had little to do—for example, when Veronica was being tutored. And since Polly had an easy life in the house, being forced to fetch and carry all day, in Mrs Jenkins view, was a punishment.

For Veronica, it was perfect.

It meant she could remain in her nightdress which, given the heat, was a delight. She wore nothing beneath it and the air circulating across her body was quite delicious.

And then there was Seth's parting shot about a Faraday—he had been referring to the Faraday device. What a bright fellow he was to think of it. If she had a Faraday under her bed it would mean she would weigh less than half what she did normally. As a result, the strain on her back would be considerably reduced. It would give her respite through the night.

She was so taken with the idea, it quite drove her intentions on Polly's body from her thoughts.

She went to the window and let the sun play across her while she looked out. Seth was not in view.

The problem was electricity: the house had none. It was not uncommon for grand houses to have their own generators nowadays, usually for the purpose of lighting. But Versyns Hall was not large, and since her parents were hardly ever in residence, and never entertained when they were, it was not a priority. Probably not even a thought—she could not recall the last time she had seen her mother or father.

She sighed loudly. There was no way this side of Judgement Day she could get the house equipped with electricity, let alone get herself a Faraday grid for her bed.

"Is there something wrong, miss," said Polly from where she sat, re-attaching a piece of lace which had torn away where it caught on Veronica's heel when they had been walking.

"Seth raised my hopes and now they are dashed."

"I don't understand, miss."

"A Faraday under my bed would be a tremendous boon to my sleeping, but it is quite impossible to power one."

"I don't even know what one is, miss."

"It is the device that allows the British to rule the skies as we once did the waves, Polly. You must have heard of it."

Polly shrugged. "Can't say I have, miss."

Veronica jumped at a knock on the door. In the first place no one ever knocked and, in the second, she was not expecting to be disturbed.

Without thinking she called out. "Enter."

She turned towards the door with the sun at her back, just as Polly looked up in horror. "But, miss..."

Through the opening door peered Mr Plumley. "Oh, my," he said as he saw her. Several books and his portable writing desk crashed to the floor. But he did not look away. His gaze was glued to her frame. Not even her face.

Moments later, Polly materialised between them and threw Veronica's dressing gown across her back. "Do it up," she hissed. "You're showing everything, miss."

For a moment Veronica had no idea what she was talking about, or why Mr Plumley had reacted so. Then she realised. The sun was behind her and would be shining through her nightdress, revealing every curve of her body—including her hump—as if she were one of the statues that adorned the house. Not that any of those had a spine deformity. They were all perfect.

Veronica fumbled with the belt and managed to tie a knot. She knew she ought to feel embarrassed, but she did not. Mr Plumley had gathered up his things and backed out of the door. He was now trying to close it without dropping them again.

"Please, Mr Plumley, it's all right now. I am decent," she said as she sat in the hardback chair by the window, but out of the sun. "But I don't understand, why are you here?"

"I am p-paid to teach you, Miss Clifford-Hughes. I understand you had a f-fall?"

"Nothing serious, sir."

"Then we m-must c-continue your lessons."

And that was that. Her hopes for a quiet day were shattered.

Polly was sent to find two male staff while Veronica hid herself from view in the dressing room. Her bedroom had no table or desk suitable to work on so one needed to be brought. There was a chair in the small space but it was dark and the room had no method of illumination—though if they had the electric it could. Light seeped through the gap at the bottom and her eyes adjusted.

As she sat there listening to the sounds in the room, almost of its own volition, her right hand slipped inside her dressing gown and gently manipulated her breast and nipple. Now that things had settled down, her frustration at not reaching the pinnacle of lust that morning visited her. The idea that three men might catch her touching herself in such a wanton way was quite stimulating.

She mused as to whether her lack of embarrassment—indeed more than a lack of embarrassment, more a desire to be observed—was a deficiency in her moral fibre. No doubt Mrs Jenkins, Mr Laughton the Steward, and Reverend Peacock would think so, but that only made her feelings of rebellion intensify and she gave her nipple a particularly vicious tweak.

Once the staff were gone, Polly came in and the light dazzled her.

"Shut the door," said Veronica in a whisper, she had an unresolved idea and was acting without thinking. As Polly pulled it to, Veronica stood up and caught a glimpse of the back of Mr Plumley's jacket. The desk had been set-up close to the window and he was in bright sunlight.

The room went dark again, and Veronica was blind. She reached out to find Polly's wrist, she missed and her hand landed on her maid's waist. Good enough. Veronica took a small step forward and slid her hand to the small of Polly's back then pulled her closer. Polly did not resist. Veronica's nose bumped into Polly's forehead, and the bruise throbbed slightly. Veronica ignored it, she had a different target in mind.

She traced a line down Polly's face, she found her eye and moved slightly to follow the nose. Until she could feel Polly's breath on her own lips. Her heart was pounding. The stories told of kisses between men and women. Never one about a kiss between women. Why not?

She wondered whether she should ask permission, but Polly had not pulled away. Veronica closed the gap and her lips tingled as they touched Polly's. The feeling was, in its uniqueness, as stimulating as when Polly had stroked her nipples. Veronica had never kissed anyone before, there had barely even been a peck on the cheek.

Even though it was dark she closed her eyes and pushed her lips harder against Polly's. Their noses touched side by side. The tenseness went out of Polly and she relaxed into Veronica's embrace. Her arms encircled Veronica in return. Their bodies pressed together, and the pressure on Veronica's already stimulated breasts added to the intense mix of sensations.

Then Polly's lips separated, and they were pressed so tight against Veronica's that hers could only follow suit. Veronica breathed Polly's breath. She could barely contain herself, she desperately wanted to moan but dared not in case Mr Plumley heard them. What would he think if he knew? The thought excited her.

She almost jerked her head back when Polly's tongue darted into her mouth like a heron spearing a fish. Veronica opened her eyes wide in surprise. They had adjusted to the dark again and she could see Polly's eyes looking back at her. They seemed to be laughing.

Tongues? Veronica could not imagine that something that might seem so ... strange, could be so interesting. Polly's tongue explored her mouth, running along her teeth and touching her own tongue. Stabbing at it. Veronica tentatively pushed back and Polly's retreated. Veronica followed and found herself exploring the maid's mouth with her tongue. Her whole body tingled, as if she were going to paroxysm, yet it seemed far away.

She was not aware of how long they remained clinging to one another, tongues exploring and duelling, but eventually Polly withdrew her tongue and closed her mouth.

"We must stop, miss," she said quietly, although Veronica could hear the lust in her voice, and the way she breathed quickly. Just as Veronica was.

Then Polly dropped one hand to Veronica's behind, spread her fingers and squeezed. Veronica grunted. And was entirely astonished at the sound she made, as well as the feelings that had shot through her and, most of all, the effrontery of the maid to do such a thing. And after that the knowledge that the touching of the rear end could also be exciting.

Polly giggled so quietly the sound barely reached her mistress's ear, let alone Mr Plumley's. Then she stepped away and Veronica's arms slid from her. Polly paused for a moment, as if composing herself, opened the door and light flooded in.

Once her eyes had adjusted Veronica could see the red flush across Polly's cheeks. Veronica glanced into the mirror by the door. She was showing more skin than her maid and her flush spread across her chest and up to her ears, as if she were consumed by a fever. Yet she felt more alive than she ever had before.

Polly adjusted her wrap so that it fully covered her from neck to wrist, giving time for Veronica's lust to settle to a gentle simmer.

xi

It took until the third time Mr Plumley had to retrieve his elegant Birmingham-made fountain pen from the floor—where it had either rolled, or he had knocked it—for Veronica, who was reading a particularly dry commentary on Plato (written in French), to realise he was doing it deliberately.

They were both seated at the newly arrived table, with matching chairs that were a little too tall for her. As a result her feet dangled an inch from the carpet and her slippers had fallen off. She was well aware that a woman exposing more than her hands and face was considered a sign of low character but she was not expecting anyone to notice.

It seemed Mr Plumley had indeed noticed, and was giving himself reasons to observe her feet.

That was interesting. She glanced across at Polly, who was looking at the man on his hands and knees under the table. Polly raised an eyebrow and grinned.

Veronica had a mad thought. Pretending she had an itch, and despite the protest from her spine, she lifted her right foot and reached down to scratch her calf. In doing so she lifted the material of her nightdress, pulling it up her left leg to reveal her ankle and much of her calf on that side.

There was a bang as Mr Plumley's head struck the underside of the table, and he emitted a pained groan.

Polly's hand went to her mouth to hide her grin, though her eyes were wide with mirth. Veronica allowed herself a laugh.

"Oh, Mr Plumley, are you all right?" she said and slipped off her chair. She stepped round to his side of the table and stood beside him—he was head and shoulders beneath the table. She made a point of lifting the skirt so that both feet and ankles were completely exposed.

"Are you all right, sir?" she asked again.

"I am unharmed," came the voice from below the table.

"Is there anything I can do to assist?"

"N-no." His voice seemed strained.

Veronica glanced at Polly, who shrugged but was still smiling. It occurred to Veronica that her maid had never smiled in her presence before. There had been a significant shift in their relationship since their secret kiss less than an hour ago. They were no longer mistress and servant, but co-conspirators in wantonness and deviltry.

Her thoughts were interrupted as Mr Plumley crawled backwards into the open. Her immediate urge was to back away but she resisted and remained, keeping her ankles exposed.

When Mr Plumley's head emerged it was apparent, though she could only see the developing bald patch, that his eyes were fixated on her feet.

How curious, she thought and then said. "Would you like to touch my feet?"

There was a little "oh" of horror from Polly. Mr Plumley froze.

"You can touch them," she said again. "If that's what you would like."

The words "N-no, yes" came from below her, but it sounded as if it had been uttered by a dying man suffering in extraordinary pain.

"Are you sure you are well, sir?"

"I am n-not well." This time his voice was somewhat less strained, though still he had not moved. She could perceive a rigid tension in his body, almost a quivering as if he both wished and did not wish to touch her.

"Perhaps," she said, in a conversational tone, "there is something else you would like to do with my feet?" Once again she surprised herself. She was neither horrified nor embarrassed that her tutor of many years was staring at her feet and gained some sort of pleasure from it. After so long of no attention whatsoever, all the attention she had been receiving in the past few days was like a strong wine, and she was drunk on it.

"I w-would—" his voice tailed off as if the act he wanted to perform could not be spoken.

"Please, sir, do not fear, please tell me what you would like."

"To s-smell them."

Veronica looked across at Polly who seemed fit to explode with restrained mirth. She was clearly not going to be of any use.

"You wish only to smell them?"

The hesitation before the word "yes" hissed from his mouth told her that he was not being entirely honest. However she could see no harm in permitting him to smell her feet.

"Then, please, do so."

He moved suddenly, like an animal, and she jumped, taking a step back.

"But gently, if you would be so kind."

There was a sound that may have been an apology, and he crawled more slowly towards her. His arms were bent so his elbows touched the floor and his head was close to the ground. The result was even more like an animal. He approached her feet tentatively, perhaps concerned she might change her mind. She could hear him taking quick sniffs through his nose. The bristles of his moustache tickled her toes and she could feel his breath on them.

He started at the little toe on her left foot, and with barely any distance between his nose and her skin, he worked his way to the big toe. Then moved to the other foot and worked his way from the large to the small. She could not help but think of the "little piggy" rhyme, and almost burst out laughing again.

He mumbled something.

"I beg your pardon, My Plumley?"

"Your f-feet are quite clean, Miss Clifford-Hughes."

Veronica glanced over to where Polly was sitting, thoughtfully. The maid was no longer suppressing a laugh, instead staring in astonishment. Veronica turned back to the man on his knees, worshipping at her feet.

"Tell me, Mr Plumley, which do you favour, feet that are fresh and washed, or those with a more pungent aroma?"

He cleared his throat and she could feel his words as he spoke. "As unwashed as p-p-possible."

Veronica was pleased she had divined the truth. "So an opportunity to inhale the scent of feet encased for hours in shoes in this hot weather would be a treat then?"

There was an assenting grunt from below.

"Remove your shoes and stockings, Polly."

"What?" said the maid, then added. "Miss?"

"Do as I say, Polly, remove all that is on your feet," she said in stern tone, quite unlike herself.

Polly frowned at her mistress as she busied herself removing her shoes and stockings. They certainly were pungent, Veronica wrinkled her nose at the smell even at this distance. Polly pouted angrily but she said nothing.

Veronica took a step back from Mr Plumley and bent smoothly at the knee; it was the only way she could comfortably get down to his level.

"There, sir, are two sweaty and odorous feet you may smell to your heart's content."

He set off, crawling, across the floor. Perhaps it was easier than getting up.

"But," she said, and he came to a halt. "There is something I must have in return."

For the first time, he turned his head and looked at her sideways.

"But it is something that will serve you also. I can provide you with feet to smell, perhaps even to lick," and she saw from the voracious look that flickered across his face that she had correctly identified his true desire, "but we run the risk of discovery. The door to the study below can be locked but my bedroom cannot. I require a lock on my door. A bolt."

"A b-bolt?"

"You must find a reason that will persuade them to fit one."

"And if I do?"

"I will keep my feet unwashed and encased in shoes for you to lick clean."

There was a moment's hesitation then he nodded.

"But until then, sir, no licking. You may only smell."

He was satisfied after some fifteen minutes of investigating Polly's feet. Then he returned to his chair and they continued the lessons for the rest of the day, breaking only for lunch.

He left at four o'clock.

Veronica had stood, as was polite, and escorted him to the door of her room. He had paused and glanced down at her feet. Obligingly she raised her night dress. His eyes were riveted on them until he somehow shook himself to break the spell.

"Until t-tomorrow, M-miss c-Clifford-Hughes." And with that he departed.

She pushed the door closed and leaned against it. Her back was aching from sitting so long with her feet dangling. She ran her fingers along the gap between wood and frame. Her lust was driving her, she knew. It was a fire within her, and fire, as she had been taught, was a good servant but a bad master.

It was her lust that was desperate for the bolt on the door, her desire to be able to satisfy herself without fear of being disturbed. She hoped beyond hope that he might be able to concoct a reason for a bolt.

He had queried the bolt and she had not responded but her reason was plain enough: If the lock possessed a key than it could be opened from either side. Was the temptation of her malodorous feet sufficient to drive him?

His desire was strange but, she supposed, harmless.

"What do you think?" she asked Polly. "You know so much more of the world than I do."

"I have never heard of such a thing, miss."

Polly came over to the door and stood very close to her mistress, almost touching.

"Am I very ugly?" said Veronica. "How can you even bear to be close to me?"

"You are not ugly, miss."

"Don't," said Veronica harshly, then was instantly remorseful at the pain that crossed her maid's face. More gently: "Don't call me 'miss' when we are alone, when we are being like lovers."

"What should I call you then?"

"Call me by my name."

Polly hesitated as if the years of conditioning prevented her from uttering her mistress's name. "Veronica."

"No, that feels wrong, it is too formal. It sounds like my mother or father." *When they deigned to use my name at all.* "A nickname. I have never had one. Choose one for me."

Polly pulled a face. "Von? Voni? Roni?"

Veronica laughed. "It makes me sound like a Prussian or just a man." *Though that might be interesting.*

"Nika?"

"Yes! I will be Nika, it sounds Russian and mysterious, and it does not begin with the letter V." She turned so she was facing her maid. "You must call me Nika when we are close like this." She reached both arms around her maid and pulled her the short distance so they were pressed against one another.

Polly's lips were no distance from hers and when she breathed Veronica's new name it was as if she breathed a spell into her. "Nika, shall we go into the dressing room once more?"

A wave of exhaustion overcame Veronica. She touched her lips against Polly's with the gentleness of a butterfly and then shook her head. "I do desire you, but today has been too much. My back pains me a great deal from all the sitting and my nose still aches from the fall. I feel my strength is gone, I need to lie down for a while."

Polly repaid her kiss with another. "Then I will turn down your bed and look forward to a day when we can lay together without risk of interruption."

While she went about her business, Veronica went to sit in her armchair moving around the unfamiliar table. "I will need to wear stockings and shoes tomorrow to satisfy Mr Plumley's desires."

"Of course."

"I'm sorry I forced you to let him smell your feet."

"I am bound to obey the commands of my mistress."

"I'm not sure things like that are included."

Polly was fluffing a pillow but at Veronica's words she straightened, holding it tight to her belly. Her face was deadly serious and there was a hint of sadness.

"Yes, mi-Nika, those things are included."

xii

The following morning she woke late and in pain. The twisting nausea in her belly eclipsed any ache from her nose the way the sun obliterates the stars. It was that time of the month. She groaned and turned in the bed, feeling the cursed slickness between her thighs.

She should have remembered. She was quite regular and a week ago she knew it had been due. She used a bad word. Things had been so strange and exciting since her birthday, it had not even occurred to her.

Perhaps a mechanical calendar clock connected to a Babbage machine could be designed such that people could be warned of periodic events. Perhaps someone had already invented it. How would she even know?

"Mistress?"

Polly should have remembered, she thought. Well, that meant she could proclaim herself properly unwell and Mr Plumley could stay away for a couple of days. One thing was certain, she had no interest in indulging his predilection for smelly feet.

She groaned.

"Oh," said Polly.

"Yes." The word emerged as more of a growl than anything else.

Veronica felt the bed move and the single sheet pulled off her body. Then she felt the maid's breath against her face followed by a gentle kiss on her cheek. "We'll get things cleaned up, then I'll let Mrs Jenkins know and prepare a bath."

"Everybody knows everything about me," said Veronica, surprising herself by bursting into tears. "All the servants will know. I have no privacy. It's not fair." She sniffed.

"No, miss. But at least no one will come in unannounced, or at all."

"Why does this have to happen? Our biology is so perverse."

"Yes, miss."

Then a thought occurred to Veronica. It was like a dagger through her conscience. She opened her eyes and looked at Polly kneeling on the bed beside her.

She put out her hand and touched her knee. A familiarity she would never even have dreamed of just a few days before.

"I ... have never considered you?" She hesitated. "You do have monthlies?"

Polly's laugh was so sudden and so loud Veronica cringed as if it were anger. And it was gone almost as fast. "I am a woman too."

"I'm sorry that I never noticed your pain." But at that moment she knotted up inside again. The torture of it forced more tears from her though she had ceased crying.

"Come on, up you get," said Polly gently.

"I am not a child!"

But she let herself be brought into a sitting position dreading the mess she was making on the sheets.

Polly moved away, rummaged in a drawer and then left the room for nearly twenty minutes. Veronica cried a bit in the meantime and stared at the wall.

When the maid returned, she thrust a hot water bottle into Veronica's hands. She cuddled it to her midriff, allowing the warmth to penetrate her skin and relax her spasming muscles.

"What advantage is there in being a woman?" said Veronica to no one in particular. Polly did not respond, she fetched a bowl and a flannel, and set about cleaning her mistress.

"I should do that myself, you don't have to."

"You should stop feeling so sorry for yourself."

"It hurts."

"I know. Stand up. Legs apart please."

Veronica did as she was told and sniffed again. She felt like a baby. Wasn't she capable of even looking after herself a tiny bit, that she should be waited on hand and foot—and groin. It was pathetic. She was pathetic. And an ugly hunchback.

The rubber bottle was working its magic slowly. Her stomach was less knotted up though it still ached.

"Why doesn't this happen to you?" she said sullenly.

"You would wish it on me?"

Veronica wished she hadn't spoken at all. "I didn't mean that—I just meant..."

"I know what you meant."

"I'm sorry."

"You're always this way when it comes."

"Am I?"

"Oh yes."

"Sorry."

"Hush."

Veronica hushed and let Polly complete her intimate ablutions. The maid then fetched a fresh pad, threaded it between her legs and tied it round her waist.

"I hope you made enough," said Veronica. "I think this will be a bad one."

"We'll see. I can always make more." Polly stood up and cleared away the bowl and rags. "Walk up and down for a while."

Veronica didn't argue. She knew Polly was right even though walking about was the last thing she wanted, but her urge to be contrary had already lessened with the reduction in pain.

The sheets were a mess but Polly cleared them away. She left the mattress to air after cleaning it as best she could.

As her attention became less fixated on herself, Veronica realised the sun was not shining. She went to the window and looked out. Solid banks of cloud were racing across the sky from the northwest. The trees in the garden were moving fretfully in a brisk but uncertain wind. Every now and then a warm draught blew through a gap in the window frame.

"The weather has changed."

"Yes, miss."

Polly's response was automatic; it meant she wasn't really listening.

Veronica almost felt that the experience of the last few days were nothing but her own imaginings, that perhaps she was going mad like Mr Rochester's first wife. But then she remembered Polly's morning kiss and touched her hand to her cheek as if she could still feel it.

The physical pleasures were a delightful agony, but the warmth of another human holding her because they liked her, exceeded that by far.

She remembered how good it was to hug Polly and hold her close. Though it would be a very long time before it made up for all the embraces she had never had from those who were supposed to love her. Well, if her real family could not give her what she needed, perhaps she could make a family that would. Perhaps Polly, perhaps Seth, perhaps even Ursula though she had yet to meet her.

Not Mr Plumley, though, he was a means to an end.

How Machiavellian of her.

"Do you and Ursula take pleasure in one another's bodies?" she asked out of the blue.

That Polly hesitated was enough of an answer. Then: "Ursula is very shy, miss."

"Isn't it unusual for women to lie with one another?"

"We would do so if we had a chance."

Veronica's heart leapt at that. "But still unusual."

"A woman is gentler than a man. A woman knows what pleases another woman."

"You've thought about it."

"Not me, that's Ursula, she's clever. Deserves better than being a housemaid, miss."

"Nika. Please."

"Nika."

"Did you seduce her, or the other way around?"

"It just happened."

"How?"

Polly put down her sewing and stood up. "I'll sort out the bath."

And she went away.

Veronica decided perhaps she should say nothing when it was her time of the month.

xiii

It was two days later, after breakfast, when there came a rapping on her door. The windows were open to allow the circulation of air, since rain had fallen and the humidity had increased to an unpleasant level. And Veronica was, on this occasion, fully dressed.

Her condition had meant her activities with Polly were limited to the occasional kiss and hug. Though she found that to be not only sufficient but preferable. Her lust was in abeyance.

Polly opened the door to Mr Plumley carrying his books and bag. He was accompanied by one of the male staff wearing a heavy leather apron and carrying a toolbox. The teacher came in and set his things on the table, indicating with a peremptory wave of his hand that Veronica should come and sit.

The workman set down his wooden toolbox with a solid thump on the carpet. It had a fascinating hinge arrangement so that when he opened it different levels of shelves opened such that all their contents were available. Veronica thought it most impressive.

Mr Plumley cleared his throat to attract her attention. He pushed the French commentary on Plato in front of her again. Unusually there was a piece of paper marking the page. She opened the book and extracted the bookmark, she was about to lay it to one side when she saw the writing on it.

"Have you been wearing your shoes all morning?"

Veronica kept her composure and looked up at Mr Plumley, he held a pen out. She glanced over to the man who was just measuring places on the door and making marks.

"With my woollen stockings. Is he putting in a bolt?"

She handed the note back. There was a look of pleasure, not to say expectation, on her tutor's face as he nodded.

Thank god, thought Veronica. She imagined her future freedom, lying in bed with Polly. Or lying in bed with Seth's muscled torso. Or simply lying bed naked and not having to worry about interruptions.

The anticipation was thrilling, though she would now have to go through with her side of the bargain and allow him to lick her feet. While her books were vague on the details, they did imply very bad things could happen to a woman in the presence of a man if they were alone. She did not think it involved licking feet.

In the future, if she found the need to make deals of this nature again, she must be sure to place a time limit on them. "Licking of feet each day, except Sundays, for a period not exceeding nine weeks." Perhaps setting it out in a contract where all the parties sign.

And then she giggled at the silliness of her idea, as she imagined dour-faced solicitors writing up and witnessing the contract. She received a stern look from Mr Plumley.

She found it impossible to apply herself to the French with the sound of her salvation being constructed behind her. How long did it take to install a bolt on a door?

"You are f-fidgeting, M-miss Clifford-Hughes, kindly desist," said Mr Plumley.

"I am finding it hard to concentrate with the noise."

"Then you must exercise."

She looked at him in astonishment. What was he thinking?

"P-p-pace, M-miss Clifford-Hughes, walk up and d-down. It activates the b-blood and w-warms the m-muscles. You have b-been idle and your *f-feet* need exercise."

Ah, so that was why. "Very well, sir, I shall do as you instruct. I'm sure it will help my lesson."

She left the table and paced the room from one end to the other. On the return journey she was facing Polly, whose face was calm but her eyes sparkling with a desperate need to laugh. In the end Polly went into the dressing room, claiming some forgotten task as her reason.

The other advantage of walking, apart from increasing the sweatiness of her feet and thereby the pleasure of Mr Plumley, was that she could watch the progress of the workman.

It seemed he was not applying a single bolt but two, one low down and the other near the top. Veronica was certain neither she nor Polly would be able to reach it without a step. Was it possible her teacher had deliberately chosen this configuration so that he could trap them in the room?

She played the scenario out in her mind. If he had done that in order to wrest more from her than she was willing to give there would be little she could do about it. If she complained, he would simply deny it, and she would be carted off to the asylum, or locked in a tower. The former seemed rather more likely, unfortunately.

But it was a possibility she could not ignore.

She wracked her brains as she walked. Two years ago, in a fit of generosity from her mother—that Veronica could only put down to guilt—she had been given a Kodak camera. If Polly took photographs of Mr Plumley licking her feet he would not be able to deny it.

Polly emerged from the dressing room just as the workman was finishing and packing up. He touched his forelock to her and left.

The three of them were alone.

xiv

Even if she was not excited by the thought of having her feet licked, the anticipation of what she was about to do—something utterly taboo—caused her to breathe more deeply and rapidly than usual. It was moment of great significance and she wanted it to be perfect.

She saw her tutor opening his mouth to speak.

"Hush!" she demanded, holding out her finger in an admonishing fashion and, to her astonishment, he obeyed. His mouth closed without a sound being uttered and he simply waited. The power thrilled her. "Mr Plumley, go and lock my door."

Without another word, or even an attempt at one, he stood as a man in a trance and walked across. He passed so close she felt the air move the hairs on her arms. It was like electricity.

She chose not watch as he slid home the bolts.

Even the fact that she was now at risk excited her, but she had Polly here as well and the camera could wait until next time.

She pointed at the armchair in the corner. "Sit there, sir."

Once again he obeyed and settled himself, staring at her, awaiting her next command. To Veronica it was like a dream. She glanced at Polly, whose expression was indecipherable. Veronica lifted her skirts as if she was walking in mud so her hem was above her ankles, then stepped across the room making each step large and obvious. As if it was a dance.

Mr Plumley's attention was riveted to her feet. His head moved slightly as she lifted each in turn and placed it closer to him.

Still six feet from him, she stopped. "What reason did you give them for providing bolts?"

It was with some difficulty he raised his eyes from the floor to her face. At their relative heights the curvature of her spine meant that she was looking directly at him. Somewhere in the back of her mind there was a voice telling her that staring at a man, full in the face, was the act of a shameless woman. It was already established that she was without shame, so the voice was irrelevant.

"I said that p-part of your instruction in horticulture should include xeno-b-botany." He took a deep breath and glanced once more at her feet and then back to her face. "That you would keep a n-number of specimens in your room as they require constant attention."

"And the bolts?"

"To prevent you being disturbed during any difficult procedures."

"The top one is too high for either me or Polly to reach."

"Yes, I did not specify a single b-bolt b-by the lock." He hesitated and his eyes were once more drawn to her feet where they remained locked. "I hope you do not f-feel this b-breaks our agreement." His voice quivered as he said it.

She chose not to reply to him but instead addressed her maid. "Polly, please close the windows and bring one of the chairs to me."

When she had done so, Veronica sat with exaggerated elegance. She settled, facing slightly away from Mr Plumley.

"Oh my," she said, speaking into the air, "what a tiring day it has been. My poor feet are so hot and tired. My dear little toes ache from the days walking and the evening's dancing. They must be released them from their prison."

She crossed her legs and pulled up her skirts almost to her knees.

"Dear Polly, remove my shoes and stockings."

The maid did as she was told and knelt in front of her mistress. She looked up at Veronica, who winked on the side the tutor could not see. Polly suppressed a grin.

"Oh but, mistress, your feet do stink so terrible when you've been on them all day."

"It cannot be helped. They must be exposed."

Polly made a big show of unbuckling each shoe, and held each one up to her nose. "Oh, it do stink."

In fact the odour of her feet was certainly much stronger than it had been that first day when Mr Plumley's proclivities had been discovered. Though not as bad as it could be on some days.

Next came the stockings, each garter drawn down and then the stocking rolled after it. "Smelly!" was Polly's cry.

When both had been done Veronica made a little move of the head to indicate Polly should go back to her chair near the dressing room. Veronica made a great show of pointing her toes and examining her feet.

"Oh if only they could be cleaned as well," she said, leaving the words hanging in the air. Finally she turned her head towards Mr Plumley. His mouth was open and he was salivating.

"Kind sir," she said distracting him only briefly from her toes. "Is there anything that you can do to clean my feet?" She stretched her right foot in his direction as if offering it to him.

Her tutor slid from the armchair and on to his knees, then forward to all fours, once again with his arms bent so his nose was at floor level. He crawled forwards quickly and stopped just shy of her toes. He breathed in through his nose and filled his lungs with the 'sweet' scent of her sweaty feet.

He glanced up into her face as if asking permission and she nodded.

The first touch of his tongue against her skin was a gentle dab on the top of her big toe. She did not look away but watched—though his head obscured the exact action. He lifted his head a little and she could see the glistening of the spot of saliva.

Perhaps he was waiting to see what her reaction would be, taking care not to alarm her. But she was not alarmed, not upset, merely curious—though a little apprehensive of being tickled. She was certain that jerking her foot back and laughing would spoil the whole thing.

Apparently satisfied she was not going to react badly, Mr Plumley took the next step and his tongue, with more pressure, slid from the end of her big toe, across the nail and along the full length.

Something stirred inside her. Surely not? How could this bring about lust?

He licked the outside of her big toe and then dug his tongue between the two toes, where the dirty sweat tends to accumulate. Her feelings could not be denied. She was certain it was not the licking of feet *per se* that was generating these feelings in her. It was more the mere fact of another person touching her skin in such an intimate manner.

After all, Mr Plumley's desires were directed towards the smells and taste of dirt and sweat. While she—

"Oh!" He had sucked the whole of her toe into his mouth and, in its damp warmth, he was rolling his tongue across it and under it. His saliva was a bath and, she had to admit, the whole effect was remarkably stimulating.

—While she certainly had no desire to ingest smelly feet. She could imagine herself, however, sucking Polly's dainty toes into her mouth. As long as they were clean.

He repeated the process for each toe on that foot, and then transferred his attentions to the other. Her breasts wanted to be touched. Her nipples were hard and between her legs were interesting sensations she had never explored.

Surreptitiously, so as not to alarm him, she moved her hand so she could squeeze her breasts. She realised Polly was watching her, but the maid smiled. The attention was not satisfactory since she was working through several layers of clothing (and she was not going to reveal herself to her tutor).

Once all her toes had been cleaned, Mr Plumley raised his head slightly and Veronica dropped her hand from her breast.

"M-may I clean the soles as w-well?"

"You may."

"I m-must hold your heel."

"You may handle my feet," she said, "but if it tickles too much we may have to stop."

She was surprised at how extraordinarily gentle he was as he cupped one hand behind her heel and lifted. Unfortunately he had to lift quite high and it was a strain on her back. For now she put a brave face on it, after all, he deserved a reward for his success with the bolts. She slid forwards until she was perched precariously on the edge of the chair to accommodate his needs.

Initially he tackled the area at the base of her toes where he had not been able to reach before. Then moved to the ball which, she noted, was not very sensitive composed as it was of hard skin. The softer areas, however, were very sensitive and she had to suppress the impulse to pull away.

"The soles of your f-feet are different," he said as he finally set back on his heels in front of her and released her. She pushed herself back upright. His tone was conversational, almost as if he had not spent the last half an hour sucking her toes.

"In what way?" she said.

"The areas of hardness, the p-pressure p-points, are in different p-places."

"My condition forces me to walk in an unbalanced fashion," she said. "Have you licked many feet?"

He sighed as he clambered to his feet and went back to the armchair. "N-not as m-many as I would like, M-miss Clifford-Hughes."

Almost without hesitation she said. "Under these conditions, Mr Plumley, I would like you to refer to me as Mistress Nika."

"M-mistress N-nika?"

"Yes, when you are teaching me I am Miss Veronica Clifford-Hughes, but at times like this, Mistress Nika."

He nodded. "V-very w-well, M-mistress N-nika."

XV

"We cannot do this every day, Mr Plumley," Veronica said as her tutor was packing his things ready to leave. He had not demurred when she asked him to unlock the door—after Polly had helped her back into her shoes and stockings.

"I understand."

"Perhaps twice a week? Would Wednesdays and Saturdays suit you? It would give my feet time to achieve a good level of ripeness."

She could see in his eyes that he was torn, on the one hand he wanted it to be more often, on the other was the opportunity to have *tastier* toes. She understood because it was a form of lust, if directed in a curious way. Satisfying it all of the time would reduce its potency, while anticipation was almost as delightful as the action itself. But with today being Wednesday it meant he would not have her feet again for three days.

He nodded with reluctance. It came to her that she could refuse him and there was nothing he could do about it. He was ruled by his desire and as long as the possibility of having it so easily satisfied was there, he would obey her instructions.

"Until my lesson tomorrow then, sir."

"Goodbye," he said, then added quietly. "M-mistress N-nika."

The door closed behind him. The sound of rain battered the window for a few moments and then subsided. Veronica looked out in surprise at the misty greyness that had descended.

"*Mistress* Nika?" said Polly after a few moments of silence, jerking Veronica's attention back into the room.

"I don't know," said Veronica. "It seemed appropriate. Have you noticed how he does exactly what I say?"

"I don't know how you let him do it at all."

"He did something for me, I did something for him." She walked across to the desk. There was her own pen and some paper left for her. She sat and arranged the paper in front of her, and checked the pen was charged with ink.

"What is Seth's surname?"

"The gardener?"

"Of course, the gardener, what other Seth do I know?"

"Otley."

"Do you think he can read?"

"I expect he can read as good as I."

Veronica knew that Polly could read reasonably well; it had become law in the last ten years that every child in Britain must receive basic language and arithmetic skills. As a great industrial nation these things were important.

That's what it said in the newspapers anyway. The Whigs objected, of course, concerned that if the lower classes became educated they would become dissatisfied with their lot and rise up in revolution. But the Tories had won the day in Parliament. Schools were established and although not every child received the education they were due, most did.

"You're going to write him a letter?" said Polly. Her astonishment was plain.

"And you will deliver it."

"There'll be hell to pay if I'm caught, what you going to say?"

Vanessa turned with a frown. "I am not used to be cross-examined by my maid."

Polly hesitated and her face reddened slightly. She directed her gaze to the floor. "I thought we were more than that."

Veronica forced the sudden anger down inside and got up, though it pained her back; she gripped the edge of the table and lowered herself to her knees.

"What you doing?"

Veronica could only see the bottom of Polly's black skirt. "I am asking for forgiveness."

The skirt she could see rushed forward and gently pulled her to her feet. "The door's not locked, miss. And I spoke out of turn."

"No, I spoke out of turn. Can you forgive me?"

"It's not a maid's place to forgive her mistress. It's my duty to do as I am told."

Veronica smiled a little. "Then I instruct you to lock us in."

The maid curtsied and went to the door where she applied the lower bolt. She stretched up but her hand was a good six inches from the upper one. She glanced around then went into the dressing room and fetched out the hard-backed chair. Veronica joined her and held the back of the chair, and Polly's hand as she climbed up, slid the bolt home, and then down again.

She jumped lightly down to the carpet.

Veronica had not released her hand and pulled her close into a kiss. She breathed in through her nose, capturing the lavender scent from Polly's hair.

"You smell better than my feet."

"Shall we go to your bed?" said Polly.

Veronica pulled a face. "I have not stopped flowing yet and I really do not feel amorous."

Polly nodded and placed her head into Veronica's shoulder. "You were writing a letter to Seth."

"Yes, I must finish that."

It was impractical to walk with the two of them in so close an embrace, so she took Polly's hand and led her to the table. As if she were a gentleman, and Polly was her lady, Veronica seated her maid and then sat herself.

"I'm going to write something about the greenhouse and asking if he could prepare it."

"You can't do that," said Polly.

"Why not?"

"He is only an under-gardener, you cannot bypass the chain of command. It would cause Seth great difficulties. You must write to the Head Gardener, Josiah Otley."

"Is that his father?"

"Grandfather."

"Can he read?"

Polly shook her head. "He'll probably get Seth to read it to him."

"I better not put an apology in it then."

"What apology?"

"For not being at the window so he can look at my body."

Polly's look of shock was replaced by understanding. "So you weren't just opening the window?"

Veronica explained. Her maid's face went through various different emotions ending in laughter. "No wonder you didn't mind him being in the room when you were naked," she said. "And little wonder he was up that ivy as if the devil was behind him." She laughed again. "He'll be desperate to know what's happened."

"You can tell him."

Polly looked doubtful but nodded and was silent while Veronica composed her letter. It contained nothing incriminating so, once the ink had dried, she simply folded it.

Her back was aching with all the exertions of the day so she let Polly remove her shoes before moving to lie on the bed. Polly arranged the pillow under her to reduce the strain. Now that the idea for the Faraday had been implanted in her mind, she could not let it go, the pleasurable thought of how much more comfortable she could be.

But it was hopeless. She might have been able to arrange a bolt on her door—through judicious, not to say licentious, bribery—but to equip the house with electricity? Impossible. She would probably have bribe Mr Laughton *and* Mrs Jenkins. Heaven knows what they might want.

Polly disappeared for over an hour and Veronica dozed. She was woken by the smell of cooked meats and the door bolt being thrown once more.

The bed moved as Polly sat on it.

"For better or for worse," said Veronica into the sheet, "you have seen and touched every inch of my body at one time or another. But I have never seen more than your hands and face."

"Are we mistress and servant, or Polly and Nika?"

"What do you mean?"

"Are you ordering me to remove my clothes, or asking to see the body of your lover?"

"Um..."

"Do I have the right to say no?"

"Yes."

Polly said nothing more. From the corner of Veronica's eye, as she lay face down on the bed, it looked as though the girl was looking inward. Finally Polly pushed herself off the bed. "Come and sit in the chair."

"Like Mr Plumley."

"Yes, like him. Don't say anything, and do what I say when I tell you."

"Oh, come—"

"Nika! You want to see my body, it's my rules."

Veronica shut her mouth in surprise at Polly's harsh tone.

xvi

"Stand up, Nika."

She obeyed awkwardly, for it was easier for her to move backwards and she ended up on the opposite side of the bed. She made to go towards the armchair.

"Wait."

And stopped again. Confused.

"This is difficult for me, Nika, mistress."

Veronica opened her mouth but swallowed her question when Polly raised her hand.

"If I am going to do this for you," she said, "it is because I choose to. You may not demure at exposing your body to anyone. It is not the same for me."

Veronica nodded.

"Sit," said Polly, "please."

Her maid helped her by placing a cushion at the base of her spine as Veronica took up her position. Polly's proximity left the scent of lavender hanging in the air.

Polly stood a short distance away, close to the bed, and glanced at the locked door as if to reassure herself. There was the question of what would happen if someone knocked when Polly was in a state of undress, but Veronica would simply take the blame for any delay on to herself.

There was a moment of indecision, then Polly raised her arms and removed the pins that held her cap in place. It came away and her straw-coloured hair tumbled down to her shoulders. The shoes were next, Polly sat on the edge of the bed to remove them.

Her feet were not a revelation since Veronica had seen them before. They were quite dainty but their smell filled the room. Veronica smiled but remained silent as she had been instructed.

"Think what Mr Plumley is missing," said Polly.

Her white embroidered pinny was next and then she stopped. Polly licked her lips and looked everywhere except at Veronica herself. It was difficult to wait, and difficult to see the woman who was now her lover in such a state.

"You don't have to."

"Hush," snapped Polly. "You are so disobedient, you would make a terrible maid!"

But Veronica's comment seemed to be the spur Polly needed. Glaring into Veronica's eyes she raised her hands to where the black dress covered her neck and unpinned the brooch. Then she attacked the buttons that ran all the way from neck to hem.

Polly's throat was revealed, her skin pale. She was so beautiful Veronica wanted to tell her to stop so that she could take in the image. She desperately wanted to be the person unbuttoning the dress.

The gap at the top widened and Polly's collarbone came into view. Then the top of her white cotton chemise. Veronica held her breath and leaned forward as Polly's hands reached the level of her breasts. Without thinking Veronica reached up and pressed her palm against her own. Polly noticed the movement and she stopped unbuttoning.

"No, don't touch yourself. Stay still."

Like a child caught stealing another biscuit and being forced to put it back, Veronica dropped her hand back into her lap. The sensations between her legs had begun again. She would have to investigate—but not now.

Satisfied Veronica was behaving herself, Polly continued down the length of her dress. There were a lot of buttons. The two sides parted but the chemise was bunched and Veronica could barely make out the shape of Polly's breasts.

As she reached the last few buttons, and had to lean over to reach them, Polly turned away. With her back to Veronica she stood straight and pulled back the dress. The bunches of cloth rested at her sides and Veronica could only imagine the maid's exposed body.

Polly shrugged her shoulders and the dress fell from her shoulders but stopped halfway down her back since Polly's arms were still in the sleeves. But Veronica took in her delicately curved shoulders, the bones beneath the skin stood out. And there was her spine.

Veronica felt strange.

The only spine she was truly familiar with was her own, and it bulged at the height of the shoulder blades. It was her curse. But now she looked upon a perfect spine. Each vertebra a low hill running straight and elegant from neck down—though the back of the chemise hid it from sight. Polly was perfectly formed. As God had intended womankind to be.

Her vision blurred as Polly wriggled her arms free of the sleeves and the dress fell to the floor. Veronica knew her friend had given her a gift and stood before her wearing nothing but chemise, bloomers and stockings.

But she could not see them for the tears.

The white ghost-like shape that was Polly turned. Her arms held up like a dancer made her look like a bird to Veronica's moist eyes.

"What's wrong?" cried Polly and dashed over. She knelt beside the chair, pulled the kerchief from Veronica's pocket and dabbed at her cheeks. Then she thrust it into Veronica's hand. "Wipe your eyes and blow your nose."

Veronica wanted to protest but her instructions were to be silent so she simply did as she was told.

Polly's eyes were blue. She had not noticed before, before now all she had seen was the monochrome uniform. She had freckles on her face from the summer sun. And from where she crouched by the chair, she looked up with concern.

"Why are you crying, Nika?" she said gently.

"You are so beautiful and so perfect, while I am a hideous monster. Why should I be ashamed of exposing my body to the world when there is nothing of value to see? But you should hide your perfection and protect it."

Polly frowned. "There is nothing beautiful about self-pity."

"Your back is perfect, mine is deformed."

"That's enough," said Polly. "You will never say that about yourself again, Nika."

"But—"

"Ever."

Veronica kept her mouth shut.

"Very good," she said. "You interrupted me and we were getting to the interesting bit."

"Sorry."

Polly placed her index finger on Veronica's mouth. "Silence. I do not mind if you think I'm perfect—I'm not—but no more selfish comparisons, this is my gift to you. Just enjoy what you see."

She stood and walked back to where the dress lay like a pile of coal on the floor. Veronica could see the shape of her behind under the bloomers. Polly turned, composed herself, crossed her arms and gripped the hem of the chemise and in one swift motion pulled it up and over her head.

Cones. Polly's breasts stood out from her chest. They were not large and the area around the nipple was only slightly darker than the surround skin, just the size of a penny. Her nipples stood proud and they too were smaller than Veronica's. *No comparisons*, she admonished herself. Polly was like one of the Grecian statues.

Veronica realised that Polly was waiting for her to finish cataloguing the qualities of her chest. When Veronica sat back once more Polly turned to face the other way. Her spine was perfect like the rest of her.

Polly's hands dropped to her waist and she slipped her thumbs into the top of her bloomers. Veronica held her breath. Polly pushed slowly down. It was as her hip bones became visible that Veronica realised that perhaps her maid was not receiving enough nutrition. But that thought was washed away as the top of Polly's posterior came into view.

The bloomers slipped down across the bulge and then fell into a pile at her feet. The shadow of the crease deepened into the forbidden place between Polly's legs. Veronica remembered to breathe in, then frowned. Polly was doing something with her hands at the front of her body where Veronica could not see.

She desperately wanted to say something but knew she would be told off—and she did not want to interrupt what was happening. Polly's head went back and she made a little moaning noise. Just like Veronica did when she was stimulating herself.

Oh.

Veronica could barely contain herself. Her lust was rising and she wanted to see what Polly was doing with her hands. In particular while one hand was at breast height, the other was down between her legs and Veronica could see her fingers moving there. The sensation between her own legs grew considerably stronger and her fingers wanted to go there. Only two things prevented her, she was still wearing a pad, and Polly had said she must only watch.

In her mind Veronica implored her lover to turn so she could see what she was doing.

But she didn't. She made regular insistent guttural sounds. Then her hips moved, gyrating in a way that Veronica was sure she could not emulate. In her mind, Veronica was screaming at Polly.

Then she did turn but moved to the bed where she reclined with her right leg, knee up, on the bed and the other on the floor.

"Come closer," gasped Polly. "Look. No touching!"

Veronica wanted to remove her clothes but she was not permitted. She stood unsteadily and crossed the distance carefully. Her head was spinning with desire, and intense curiosity. She knelt beside the bed.

Polly was moving her left hand between her breasts alternately squeezing and pulling, sometimes scraping her nails across the skin. But Veronica's eyes were glued to what her right hand was doing. It moved like a steam piston, rubbing her secret delta. The hair between her legs was the same shade as that on her head and did not hide the crease between. It was moist and glistened in the light. The fleshy outer lips were open revealing another pair between, and there was a bump near the top where Polly concentrated most of her attention. Though occasionally her fingers would wander to other parts and rub those too.

Veronica did not know what she was seeing. That it was giving Polly the most intense pleasure was unquestionable. The scent arising from that source was also unmistakable, different to her own but certainly what she had smelled on Polly that earlier time. The admonition not to touch was wise since Veronica had no idea what she would do.

Instead she watched in awe as Polly reached a level of paroxysm that Veronica could barely imagine. Polly clamped her mouth shut as she screamed her pleasure. Even so Veronica was concerned someone might have heard.

Then it all slowed down. Polly ceased pulling at her breasts and simply rested her hand on one. The one between her legs moved gently and slowly. No longer touching the bump but simply around the sides until she ceased altogether.

And sighed.

Veronica swallowed, then stood and returned to the chair, still in a state of bemusement over what she had witnessed. The wetness between her own legs was more than she had ever experienced.

Polly lay for several minutes in the same position while her breathing slowed. Eventually she pushed herself into a sitting position and faced Veronica.

She put her head on one side and smiled. "There."

Veronica smiled in return but kept quiet.

Polly laughed. "It's all right, Nika, you can speak freely now. In fact say whatever you like, I'm exhausted."

"I don't know what to say."

"Thank you?"

"Thank you for your gift." She hesitated. "I did not know you could do that."

"What?"

"Between the legs."

"Haven't you wanted to?"

"Yes, sort of, but that's where all the dirty things come from."

"And more pleasure than you can imagine."

"You are beautiful."

Polly gave a tired smile. "Yes, I know, it's my curse. Many a man has told me of my beauty, before they try to take what they think is rightfully theirs."

"I don't understand, Polly."

"Not now, my love, I'm tired. Let me get dressed and we will sort out the room—I have made your counterpane damp—we'll talk later."

xvii

B ut they did not talk later.

Someone came to the house. Several someones. Polly burst into the bedroom carrying luncheon on a big tray.

"Lord Jameson is here."

"What? Why?"

Polly put down the tray in a hurry, and tea slopped over the edge of the cup.

"Mrs Jenkins says you have to come down."

Veronica was speechless. What possible reason could they have for wanting her presence, and why would the local Lord be visiting at all when her parents were not here. As far as she knew he had never visited before.

She had read in the financial sections that the lord had recently been appointed to the Cabinet. He owned considerable estates not to mention his armaments business. The papers talked of war a great deal nowadays and Lord Jameson's stock was running high.

But why on earth would he be *here*?

"Who else has accompanied him?"

"There's someone who looks like a secretary, he's carrying a document bag, and there's another young man. Quite pale and sickly if you ask me."

"Consumptive?"

Polly pulled a face. "He wasn't coughing. Perhaps he just has a summer cold."

It still made no sense whatsoever.

"Well," said Veronica. "If my presence is required then I suppose I must go down." She started for the door.

Polly barred her way and threw the lower bolt.

"What are you doing?"

"You can't go like that."

Veronica frowned and glanced at her clothes. "Like what?"

"Well, your clothes are not fresh to begin with and they are not your best."

"My Sunday dress is far too old-fashioned."

"I know but the yellow dress you wore last week is far more appropriate."

Rain lashed the window again as Polly dived into the dressing room. Veronica looked out at the rain again, then set about loosening her clothes as best she could without Polly to help.

It took the best part of thirty minutes to change. While Veronica had no experience of dealing with guests of any sort, never minding unexpected ones, she was aware that a lady was expected to make men wait. That knowledge did nothing to lift the weight of concern and confusion from her mind.

When Polly unbolted the door Veronica had reached a level of terror. She had decided to use the walking stick because she thought it made her look more distinguished. There had been no time to wash her hair but Polly had brushed it thoroughly and pinned it back quite severely. In the long mirror she thought she looked much older.

The door was open in front of her but she was scared to move. The prospect of meeting people to whom she had never been introduced was quite distressing. Three men and one of them a peer of the realm. She gave herself an inward shake. This was preposterous, they were just men who happened by luck to be born into their station. There was no difference between them and Mr Plumley—or Seth.

Polly slid her arm under her mistress's and whispered into her ear. "Come on, Nika."

Veronica threw her a quick sad smile and got herself moving. Once that was achieved Newton's Third Law seemed to take hold and she found it easier to proceed than stop again. At the great sweeping staircase that led down into the hall, Polly walked a step ahead so Veronica could put a hand on her shoulder to help steady her on the descent.

It had been a long time since Veronica had been so acutely aware of her deformity. But now it filled her mind. She was about to be judged, and harshly.

Why did she have to be put through this? Why could she not be left alone with her lovers—or soon-to-be bedfellows?

That thought brought her to the closed double doors. The butler, a Welshman by the name of Jones, waited for her. He pushed the doors so they glided open.

Every man seated in the room stood as she walked forwards on trembling legs. It was just as Polly had said. Three men, the older a man in his fifties, his suit fitting his stout frame impeccably; the second in a well-fitting but cheap suit; and the final one being the pale fellow. He had Lord Jameson's nose but other than that there was no comparison. Where the father was generously proportioned, the son was almost skeletal.

Mr Laughton and Mrs Jenkins were both in attendance. Mr Laughton had been the last to stand, which demonstrated how he felt about Veronica's standing in the household.

Polly followed a few paces behind her mistress. It was a tricky moment in some ways, as a Lady's maid she would have every right to accompany her mistress. As a simple chambermaid she did not but no one said anything.

Lord Jameson cleared his throat introduced the gentlemen. "Miss Clifford-Hughes, I am Lord Jameson, the Viscount Launceston; my son, the Honourable Edwin Jameson; and that is Mr Slack, my personal secretary."

Veronica glanced around there was an armchair available opposite the gentlemen. Polly acquired a cushion and placed it behind her as she sat.

Lord Jameson followed her every move like a hunter while his son seemed disinterested in the entire proceedings. Mr Slack busied himself with the papers but glanced at her from time to time, though he was entirely focused on her right shoulder since he could not see her back.

"So, you're Madge's daughter."

Madge? That wasn't her mother's name, but somewhere in the back of her mind she remembered that Madge could be a diminutive for Elizabeth.

"Yes, Lord Jameson."

When addressing the Queen one used the full title once, and could then revert to Ma'am. She hoped this was a similar protocol. If she had been a normal girl she would have boarded at some fine school like Roedean and then sent to finishing school to learn the niceties of social behaviour.

All the things she needed right now, but was completely ignorant of.

Lord Jameson cleared his throat. "Get on with it, Slack."

"Sir."

The man pulled out a stack of correspondence from his case. "These letters, Miss Clifford-Hughes, are from your father to Lord Jameson and, while much of the content does not concern the matter at hand, they contain the key elements of the agreement."

Veronica frowned in confusion but did not feel she could interrupt.

"Further to that correspondence I have drawn up a contract—" He delved into his bag again and withdrew a thin folder with board covers to hold the contents straight. "—two copies of which have been duly signed and witnessed by the relevant parties. Namely Lord Jameson and your father. So the matter is settled and arrangements can begin." He looked up expectantly at Veronica.

She looked at him blankly.

"I knew she was malformed," said Lord Jameson to Mr Laughton. "But I wasn't aware she lacked for wits. This was not mentioned. We may have to reconsider the terms of the contract in that event."

Veronica felt a hot flush rise within her. "I do beg your lordship's pardon if I appear confused. However I have not been informed as to the nature of this contract."

The Viscount Launceston eyed her for a moment, then nodded. "The contract may stand, Slack. And I think we can take for granted she is intact." He turned his attention to Veronica. "Miss Clifford-Hughes, the banns will be read this Sunday in your church and you will be wed to my son Edwin a month after that."

xviii

Veronica was in a state of shock when Polly managed to get her back to her room. She sat in her armchair and stared without seeing while the maid removed her shoes and stockings.

"Married?" she said into the empty air. Then lapsed into silence again.

Polly went away and came back with a bottle. Veronica barely noticed as a glass was thrust into her hand and she drank without even thinking. The liquid burned all the way down and all the way back up as she coughed and choked.

"What in God's name is this?"

"Whiskey."

"Why would you give me this?"

"To wake you up," said Polly. "And it has done its work."

She removed the glass from Veronica's hand.

"Why didn't they tell me?"

"You're not important enough."

"I'm the bride."

"You're a daughter of the upper middle classes to be bought and sold."

Veronica thought carefully. "What did he mean by 'intact'?"

Polly did not respond. Instead, she came round in front of her mistress, pulled up the foot stool and sat on it.

"You really don't know." It wasn't a question.

Veronica shook her head.

"I never thought there'd be a day when I had to explain this to one of my betters."

"I'm not better than you, Polly, I envy everything there is about you, even if envy is a sin. It's just one to add to all the ones I've committed."

"That's self-pity again, Nika."

"Sorry."

"Do you even know where babies come from?"

Veronica shook her head. "Do you know?"

Polly smiled. "Oh yes, I know."

So Polly told her which hole in a woman's body babies emerge from. Veronica went through disbelief, horror and then fear. "But it's too small."

"You have a mother, Nika, and she had a mother, and so on to the beginning of creation. And that's where you, your mother and her mother and all the rest of them came from. It gets bigger."

Veronica shook her head and remained sceptical. "Have you seen a birth?"

"A couple."

And Veronica was forced to accept the truth. Polly talked a bit more about pregnancy and how the bleeding meant she was not going to have a child.

"Having a baby sounds horrible," said Veronica.

"Birth isn't horrible, Nika. Though it hurts more than anything you've ever known—"

"I endured a lot when they were trying to straighten me."

"—more than that. At least that's certainly the way it seems at the time but afterwards there's the baby and that makes up for everything."

Veronica was not convinced but she dropped the subject. "So how does it start?"

"That's what we need men for, why they rule us, I suppose."

Veronica looked dubious.

"It takes a man and woman to make a baby. Just as it takes a stallion and a mare. Or a ewe and a ram. A cock and a hen."

Veronica shook her head. "I don't understand."

"Noah took two of every animal into the Ark, one male and one female." Polly let her voice trail off.

"I understand what you're saying, Polly, but how does it work?"

Polly sighed and looked uncomfortable. "You know that between the legs a man is different to you and I?"

"Different how?" Every naked statue in the house had its nether regions covered.

"Where we have a hole, a man has a—protrusion. A thing." Polly stopped. She looked at Veronica's confused face. Finally the maid raised one hand and made an O with her thumb and forefinger. Then, with her other hand, she grouped her three larger fingers together and thrust them into the O.

Veronica stared. Polly pulled her fingers out and thrust them in again.

"Oh." Veronica's eyes went wide and she pointed at her crotch. "In there?"

Polly nodded. "Husbands consider it their right. He will do it to you the first night you are married. He wants you to be intact, so he's the first. So he owns you."

"And intact means?"

"Your hole has some skin across it, your maidenhead. It breaks the first time so, if you've had a man in you, it won't be there."

"Are you intact as well?"

Polly shook her head, and her eyes filled with tears. "It's not important for the likes of me."

Veronica was nonplussed as Polly folded over and sobbed into her hands. *What would Polly do if it was me crying?*

Even though she still felt raw from the shock of the marriage contract, she knelt beside her maid, put her arm around the girl's shoulder and pulled Polly in closer so the damp tears fell on Veronica's shoulder.

It seemed best to say nothing. So she just held her as the wind whipped through the cracks and rained thundered against the glass.

Polly showed no sign of ceasing and Veronica did not mind, but her knees and thighs were getting sore from the strain of being in the same position for so long. She gave her maid a squeeze. "I'll return in a moment, sit on the bed."

She managed to push herself to her feet without it seeming too laboured, and threw the lower bolt of the door. Then she fetched a glass of water. By the time she returned Polly had moved. The maid's face was red, stained with tears and her nose was running. Veronica brought out her hankie and gently wiped the tears away and then held the fine linen for Polly to blow her nose.

She had never done it for anyone else before. The effect was interesting and rather damp in this instance. She tried awkwardly to wipe Polly's nose and left a streak across her cheek.

Polly smiled, though sadly. "Let me."

She went to take the hankie but grasped Veronica's hand and pulled it to her lips and gave her knuckles a kiss. "Thank you for your kindness."

Then she blew her nose noisily which rather spoilt the mood. Veronica held out the glass of water and Polly took a drink.

"I'd appreciate something a little stronger, Nika."

So Veronica fetched the bottle and they shared a glass. Veronica still hated it but could not deny the relaxing effect.

"Something bad happened to you," she said. "I remember you said something before about everything being available if you were a servant."

"If you're a woman servant," said Polly. "Doesn't happen to the men, because they can do it to us as well."

Veronica had not had any lunch and was feeling lightheaded. This, she thought, must be alcoholic intoxication. *Doesn't seem so bad.* That was another thing the vicar liked to condemn: the demon drink.

"But you do it with Ursula."

"Not the same."

Veronica offered the glass to Polly but she shook her head. "Female staff can be fired for drinking, especially on duty."

"I won't let them. You're mine."

"There you go, you own me just like all of them."

Veronica hesitated as her thoughts seemed a little confused. "Unless you don't want to." She emptied the glass down her throat. "What happened to you?"

"When?"

"When you lost your..." the word escaped her so she gestured in the general direction of Polly's bloomers.

"Virginity?"

"Yes. Was it here?"

"It was in this house, I've not been in service anywhere else."

"What room?"

Polly frowned. "The room? I suppose it was the library. Yes, it was the library." She got a vacant look.

"Was it Seth?"

"What? No, of course not, what would Seth being doing in the library?"

Good point. "The butler, Emlyn Jones!"

"No."

"Not Mr Laughton?" Veronica giggled and realised she shouldn't have. "Sorry."

"You're inebriated, Nika."

"I never had whiskey before. I think I like it. My back's not aching hardly at all," she said in a rush, though now she came to think of it her stomach was feeling strange. "I give up. Who was it?"

"You don't want to know."

"I want to know. I want to know so I can be careful and if I get a chance I will hurt him for hurting you."

"Your father."

"I—what?" She was disturbed by the anger that was bubbling up inside her friend.

"Your father did it. Are you satisfied?"

"What? How?"

"You want the details?" Polly seemed angry and Veronica did not understand why. "I was called into the library—I thought I was going to be fired—he locked the door and told me to bend over the table."

Having no experience to compare it with, and with her thoughts confused by the drink, Veronica had trouble understanding what Polly was saying. "And you did it?"

"If I didn't I would have been out with no references. We have no choice, miss, you own us body and soul."

"But—" Veronica said again trying to comprehend "—what did he do?"

"He fucked me!"

"What's 'fucked'?"

Polly's anger dissolved. "You don't even know what I'm talking about."

"I want to understand, I *need* to understand. I'm getting married, I have to understand."

"Yes, I know."

"Perhaps if I'm not intact I won't have to get married?"

"I don't think they care. I have a friend over in the big hall, Edwin is the sixth son. They don't know what to do with him. Surplus to requirements."

"Like me."

"Your father—" Polly spat the word. "—and Lord Jameson have made some mutually beneficial business arrangement around this marriage."

But Veronica wasn't listening, her stomach was still grumbling though her head seemed to have cleared somewhat. Perhaps the whiskey hadn't been such a good idea, at least not so much.

"Show me what fucking is," she said.

"What?"

"I want to know, you show me, do it to me."

"I'm not a man. I don't have the equipment."

Veronica raised one hand and made an O with the thumb and forefinger, then she thrust three fingers from the other hand into the hole.

"Show me."

xix

"You need to get undressed," said Polly as she carried the footstool to the door then climbed on it to bolt the top.

"What if someone comes?"

Polly hesitated then laughed.

"What?"

"There's so much you don't know," she said from the stool.

"That's why I need you to teach me." Veronica was struggling to reach the ties at the back of her dress, but it was impossible. She was convinced she wouldn't have been able to do it had she a normal body, or even been completely sober.

"You know when you reach that special moment."

"Like I did when you were cleaning my breasts?"

"Tits."

"What?"

"You can call them tits, Nika, or boobies, or jugs when they're big."

"Oh. Tits, boobies, jugs," she said experimentally. "Mrs Jenkins has huge jugs."

Polly laughed. "Yes, she does. When you reach that special moment it's called 'coming.'"

Veronica looked dubious as Polly jumped down and came over. She spun Veronica round and attacked the ties. "This really is a lovely dress."

"So you *came* this morning?"

"Yes," said Polly and Veronica could hear the smile in her voice. "That was very nice, having you watching me with that look of amazement was special."

"I can't help being ignorant."

The dress came loose and Polly pulled it down to the floor, revealing Veronica's silk chemise—specially tailored for her hump—and matching bloomers. Veronica stepped out of the dress and Polly put it to one side.

"Are you sure you want to do this?" said Polly.

Veronica hadn't turned around and was staring at the window again. The clouds were so heavy it was already like twilight even though it was only mid-afternoon. The wind must have dropped because the rain was no longer beating against the panes.

"I'm sure," she said. "If it's going to happen then I want it to be by you. And if they check I'll say someone crept in through my window in the night and ravished me—is that the right word?"

"I suppose."

Still without turning Veronica put her hands inside her bloomers and pushed them down then she pushed the straps of the chemise off her shoulders and pushed it down across her body, awkwardly. She knew she had none of the grace of Polly. When she had been dressed for the meeting Polly had dispensed with the pad. A quick glance at the bloomers showed they were not stained. Veronica was glad.

"How do you want me? On the bed, or perhaps leaning over the table?"

"That's not funny."

"I thought you might want to get your revenge?"

"That's not funny either."

Veronica turned to face her maid, aware of how she stooped. "It wasn't meant to be funny, Polly. If you want to hurt me, the way my father hurt you, then I am offering myself."

"I don't want to hurt you."

"If you change your mind—"

"I won't."

"—*if* you do, I will understand."

"I won't."

Veronica gave up. "So where do you want me? I can't lie on my back the way you did this morning." *Only this morning? Seems like a lifetime.*

Polly nodded. "Get on the bed. On all fours with your bum in the air."

"I know what a bum is."

Polly laughed. "Good. Hurry up about it, Nika."

"Yes, *Mistress* Polly."

Veronica climbed up into a kneeling position on the edge of the bed and, with her feet still over the side, she let herself fall forwards until her face was in the counterpane. The alcohol had helped her muscles relax and the position did not aggravate her back for the moment.

Then Polly slapped her rump. Hard. Veronica jumped. "What was that about?"

"Mistress Polly, indeed."

Veronica laughed and settled back down again.

"Nika, move your knees further apart." Polly's voice was unlike her usual gentle tone. It possessed a hardness Veronica had not heard before, but she obliged.

The cool air moved against her behind and nether regions. The fact such private areas of her body were on display did not bother her at all. Once again she wondered whether she might have something broken inside that meant such things did not concern her.

"Your father did what he did purely for his own satisfaction," said Polly, and Veronica felt a hand touch the back of her thigh before sliding upwards and across her behind.

"Do men also ... *come*?"

"Oh yes, much quicker than we do. And they emit their seed at that moment into the body of the woman they are penetrating. It's all they want to achieve. Ursula thinks it's their sole purpose in life." While she was speaking she had run her hand back down to Veronica's thigh and then back up the other leg. Veronica shivered.

"When we become excited we make a liquid between our legs—"

"I've noticed."

"It's like oil for an engine, so that when a man puts his thing in you it moves smoothly."

"That's good."

"It would be if they gave enough time for us to prepare." Both of Polly's hands were now on her bum. They were pressing and stroking. "You're getting wet now, Nika. But men don't wait. They must perform their act right now. So they push into you as soon as they can."

"Does it hurt?"

There was a hesitation. "If you are not ready, yes."

Many times Polly had cleaned her mistress between her legs with a cloth and Veronica had thought nothing of it. But this was very different as the maid's small hands stroked across Veronica's private parts. *I do not know the words.* And then she gasped as Polly touched a place near the top and a buzzing ache shot through Veronica. *Where she was touching herself this morning.*

Rational thought left her as the lust began to rise. Without thinking Veronica shifted her weight to her left arm and slid her right arm back under herself to grab her *tit*.

"Stop it," said Polly. "You are not allowed to touch yourself. Only me. And whatever happens, don't you dare move." Polly's voice had a strange and dangerous quality.

Veronica groaned in protest, but obeyed. She moved her arm back to where it could help support her weight. She wished she could see what Polly was doing. She wished she knew the names for all the parts—

Pain ripped inside her and Veronica screamed. Only the implicit threat in Polly's early words and tone kept her kneeling there. It felt as if her body was being penetrated by a poker that thrust and twisted inside. She cried out in wordless agony as it pushed and pushed. "Stop, please, it hurts," she sobbed. "Please..."

It continued a few moments longer then the immediate pain ceased as its cause was removed. The tearing sensation lingered and it was all she could focus on. It faded to a dull ache and Veronica realised Polly was no longer touching her at all. She collapsed forwards with a sob.

She lay there with her eyes open, staring at white linen, with the sound of movement not far away. The bed moved as Polly climbed on to it. Veronica sniffed and turned her head a little more so she could see the maid.

Polly was naked, sitting near the pillows at the head of the bed. She had her arms wrapped round her legs and her chin on her raised knees. The three middle fingers of Polly's right hand were spotted with blood.

The throbbing pain between Veronica's legs had passed.

"You wanted revenge after all," she said.

Polly glanced away. "You're ready for your wedding night now."

"Unless they decide to find out if I'm intact."

There was silence from the other girl.

"Did your revenge satisfy you?"

When Polly turned back to face Veronica, she was crying. "No."

"I think, when one enacts revenge, it must be against the original aggressor, or against something they care about," said Veronica. "You know my father does not care about me. Would he care that his daughter lost her maidenhead to the hand of her maid?"

Polly shook her head. "I believe he would have enjoyed it."

Veronica reached out and placed her hand on Polly's ankle. It was curious to be touching another woman's body. Up to now she had been the one to receive. One thing she had learnt in the short time she had been exploring fleshly pleasures: it was always more exciting when that pleasure was given by another.

"I hurt you," said Polly.

Veronica pushed herself up on her knees and rested her bare behind on her heels. There was a slight twinge of pain as the action pulled at the skin between her thighs.

"You were angry," said Veronica. "The trouble with anger is that it leaks."

"It was wrong."

"Nothing can take it back." She slid her hand up Polly's leg to her knee. She brushed a tear from the maid's cheek with her knuckle and brought it to her lips. Salt.

"I'm sorry."

"I know, and I'm sorry my father even exists."

"If he didn't then we wouldn't be here."

Veronica paused. *Would that be a bad thing? To have never even been born?*

"But then you would not have been a lady's maid, and I would not have learnt about Mrs Jenkins jugs." She cupped each breast and squeezed gently. The sensation made her breathe in suddenly.

"Your boobies are so—excitable," said Polly. "I can't come from having mine touched."

Veronica thought about that. "What about Ursula?"

"I—don't know."

Veronica went back to stroking Polly's lower legs and wished she could get access to more interesting parts of her anatomy.

"You don't know? But I thought you shared a bed."

Polly looked torn as if she didn't want to say then settled on: "I'm not allowed to touch her, she only touches me."

Even Veronica, whose experience was very limited, thought this odd and said as much.

Polly shrugged. "She was very kind after your father did what he did and she makes me feel very good. I do not question her rules."

"Doesn't she want to come?"

"I do not think she ever has in my presence."

Veronica smiled. "I would like to learn how to make you come. I want to show you I do not hate you for what you did."

Polly smiled with a slight twitch of her lips. Veronica pushed herself up and leaned forward, resting her hands on Polly's knees. She could not quite reach her lover's lips so settled for the tip of her nose.

Without warning Polly opened her legs and Veronica fell forward. Polly let herself fall back into the pillows with Veronica on top of her. The sensation of her flesh pressed against the bare skin of the other woman sent shivers through Veronica. The closeness was another new experience. Her head rested between the pointed hills of Polly's chest and she savoured the sound of another person's heartbeat.

Her hands were at Polly's hips and her belly against the maid's sex. The downy hairs made no impression but the mound pressed into her.

"I wish we could stay this way forever," said Veronica. Then froze as Polly's hand came down on her back. Veronica was suddenly and terribly aware of her hump. Polly's hand wandered across the spine and ribs. It followed the overly pronounced curve and then spread out to stroke the taut skin.

"If you want me to get off you, I will understand," said Veronica.

In response Polly's other hand landed on her back and, without too much pressure, held her tight.

"You are no monster, Nika."

XX

“But you're not going to learn very much lying on top of me.”

Veronica agreed, and the truth was that the position was aggravating her spine. She pushed and managed to kneel up again. It sent shooting pains through her back but it was nothing she wasn't used to and they subsided quickly.

Polly remained lying where she was, once more revealing her naked body to her mistress. This time, however, the secret place between her legs was open and on display.

Veronica was embarrassed; not for herself, but for her maid. It must have been obvious because Polly smiled.

“Give me your hand, Nika.”

She took the one Veronica held out by the fingers and guided them down between her legs. “This would be easier with a mirror but I'm sure we can manage.” The look on her face was devilish and Veronica smiled back.

“There are lots of words for a woman's privates, some less kind than others. The whole thing—” She demonstrated by touching Veronica's fingertips to the first crease at the top then dragging them down to the hole at the bottom. “—is called the quim or the muff. Sometimes a man will call a woman a quim. That is an insult. They also say cunt which is also an insult.”

Polly released Veronica's fingers and lay back. “Men are the ones who name the parts of our body. But we can give them names too if we wish. On each side there are lips, outer ones and inner ones.”

Veronica pushed her own knees apart, and as she ran her fingers gently down both sides of Polly's quim she copied the action with herself—almost as if she doubted they would be the same. A part of her was convinced she would be an abomination there as well.

She discovered she was, at least, similarly structured and the pleasure it seemed to give her maid was the same as she felt herself. She rubbed gently up and down a few times.

“Not too lightly,” said Polly. “It can tickle.”

Veronica moved to the two inner flaps of skin and a tremor went through Polly's body as the fingers moved between them. Because she could not move her knees very far apart, Veronica found herself just running her fingers between the outer lips. She would check the details later with a mirror. It didn't matter, for now it was producing a very powerful effect.

Polly almost purred with pleasure. "That's very nice, Nika. But now down to the hole."

Veronica slid her fingers down until she was touching the slightly open hole.

"Put one finger in."

"I don't want to hurt you."

"You won't, but do it slowly."

Some moisture, Veronica was unsure where it had come from, had collected on Polly's quim, and remembering the earlier instruction, she rolled her index finger around until it was damp and then frowned in concentration as she pushed gently against the soft opening.

Polly groaned. Veronica glanced up but her maid's eyes were closed and there was a smile on her face as she massaged her own breasts. Veronica suffered a slight temptation to instruct her to stop. But here she was the student and not the teacher.

The hole offered a slight resistance as if it were clamped against intruders but with only the slightest additional pressure Veronica's finger moved into the warm and moist interior. The sensation as her finger was enveloped was astonishing.

"How far do I go?"

"As far as you can," said Polly with an urgent tone to her voice. "And move it: in and out, in and out."

Veronica pushed and her finger slid inside Polly's body until it was completely swallowed. The interior seemed to have many ridges and bumps. It was such a strange thing to watch and yet her heart pounded.

"In and out!" said Polly again and Veronica obeyed, slowly at first but increasing speed as she gained in confidence. Her maid groaned again and her knees tried to pull together, but Veronica herself prevented it.

Polly gave a little squeal. "Another finger."

The effect she was having encouraged Veronica all the more. She pulled out her index finger—Polly made a disappointed sound—then with two fingers as one she thrust back in. With small motions at first and then bigger ones the maid gyrated her hips and rather than Veronica pushing into Polly, it was the servant who pushed her body on to Veronica.

Then, without warning, Polly stopped. She was panting heavily and a rosy blush had bloomed across her chest, neck and cheeks.

"Now," she panted, "at the top." With her free hand—the one that was not clutching a breast—she pointed at her quim. In the centre, where a fleshy bulb had grown and slipped from under a hood of skin. "The nubbin. All pleasure is there."

Veronica remembered how, that morning, Polly's fingers had flown back and forth across that spot. With her moist fingers she reached out. Her maid's body went rigid at Veronica's touch and she was panting. A quick glance at her ecstatic face told Veronica she was unlikely to receive any further instruction. She pressed. Polly grunted. She took it between finger and thumb and squeezed as one might a grape. Polly moaned. She twisted it. Polly cried out.

It did not seem there was any action that did not do other than stimulate this organ but she felt it best to do what she knew was right. She fanned out her fingers and rubbed them across the nubbin such that there was a short interval between each impact.

Polly responded by thrusting her hips up. Veronica moved her hand backwards and forwards, picking up speed. Polly's muscles tremored and shook, and the girl cried out on each gasp. Veronica was concerned about the noise but intended to bring her maid to the summit of pleasurable agony. On a whim, since she had a free hand, Veronica pushed two fingers into Polly's hole. The action elicited another grunt from the girl. Veronica tried three fingers and found they also would fit—the entrance was accommodating.

Her fingers were a blur across the nubbin and she thrust regularly with her other hand. Within moments Polly's back arched. She lifted herself up so only her feet and shoulders were in contact with the bed. The angle was awkward and Veronica grabbed the nubbin as best she could and squeezed while slamming her fingers in and out of Polly's hole.

The muscles enclosing her fingers spasmed, gripping again and again while Polly made little mewling sounds like a cat. She held the arched pose a few moments more and then simply collapsed back on to the bed.

"Stop, stop, stop," she whimpered. "Don't touch me, it's too much."

Veronica gently pulled her hands away. Polly's muff was running with liquid and Veronica's hands were wet with it. She brought them to her nose and sniffed. It was not an unpleasant smell; in fact, it was clearly the source of the scent of lust.

Polly's breathing was slowing and her body relaxing. Finally she opened her eyes and smiled.

"Thank you," she said. "That was very good. I think you are naturally skilled."

"You reached the peak?"

"Couldn't you tell?" said Polly with an exhausted laugh.

Veronica smiled and nodded. "I suppose so. You're very wet." She held up her fingers.

"I'll have to change the counterpane."

"Oh no," said Veronica. "I want to smell you as I go to sleep and when I wake up."

Polly just smiled and let her head fall back on to the pillow.

"I'll get some water," said Veronica. "And when you're recovered, I can do it to you again."

"Oh god," said Polly.

xxi

It had been another wet and windy morning. Veronica had not opened the window to expose herself to Seth, though he had paused with his wheelbarrow. He had been wearing a strange sort of leather cloak and hood against the weather.

She had stood at the window showing her boobies ... tits? She wasn't sure which word she preferred. So he had smiled, hopefully understanding the weather prevented their usual activities.

Polly had arrived half an hour earlier than usual and climbed into bed with her. The maid's tongue had started in Veronica's mouth but then proceeded down to her nipples. Veronica came quickly though not as explosively as she had before. In return she rubbed Polly's nubbin until she also came.

Veronica liked this new arrangement but the spectre of her upcoming marriage haunted her. In a month everything would be turned upside-down once more.

After breakfast she had been summoned to the drawing room once more. Mrs Jenkins was in attendance. Veronica looked at her jugs. Despite being constrained by her uniform they did seem to be very large indeed. It was difficult to estimate. Veronica wondered whether Mrs Jenkins had lustful thoughts and whether she was able to come just by someone touching her breasts.

She suppressed a giggle as she imagined herself sucking Mrs Jenkins tits.

However, it was Mr Slack who commanded her attention.

"The arrangements of the marriage are quite simple," he said. "You will marry the Honourable Edwin Jameson on Monday 15th August next. The wedding breakfast will be here. Edwin Jameson will take over the running of this household and it will become his estate."

"Will my parents be here?" asked Veronica.

"The event will be private and there will be no guests save the witnesses, who will comprise myself and one of my staff, Mrs Jenkins here and Mr Laughton."

"No guests? What about the bridesmaids and the best man? The groom's parents?" Veronica glanced sideways at Mrs Jenkins, who said nothing and did not even react. If truth be told, Veronica was surprised she had not been told to hold her tongue.

"You may choose one bridesmaid," said Mr Slack by way of concession. "There will be no family in attendance."

"I don't understand," said Veronica. "I appreciate that if I had disgraced myself I might be hurriedly married off in secret." Exactly like Lydia Bennett from *Pride and Prejudice*.

Mrs Jenkins did turn on her now. "You forget what you are, Miss Clifford-Hughes."

Her words stung Veronica. Their poison flowed into her blood and numbed her. A hunchback was as bad as a woman who had disgraced herself.

"If I am to be married into the nobility, I need a Lady's maid."

"You don't have one?" said Slack with the very slightest hint of surprise tempered, perhaps, by the fact that she belonged to a very lowly family—compared to Lord Jameson, anyway.

"I have one that serves in that position, but unofficially."

Slack looked at Mrs Jenkins.

There was a deafening silence from the housekeeper until finally. "It would have to be approved by my master."

Slack nodded. He had one of the modern always-ready fountain pens, from which he pulled the lid and made a note. It seemed he would perform that duty himself. Veronica decided she liked Mr Slack, for bypassing Mrs Jenkins ensured that the request would at least be honest and fair.

She could not imagine her parents caring one way or another. Wait until she told Polly about this.

Emboldened by her success, she pressed her advantage. "Do I get a wedding dress?"

If looks were daggers, Mrs Jenkins' stare would have rendered Veronica a corpse pierced by a thousand blades.

Mr Slack nodded and made another note.

"The *expense*," said Mrs Jenkins in horror.

"We will send Miss Clifford-Hughes to Lady Katherine's favourite dress designer."

"Can't they come here?"

Mr Slack looked up with a face as placid as a cow. "If it were Lady Katherine or one of her daughters, yes. However, Miss Clifford-Hughes has insufficient rank for Jeanne Paquin."

Jeanne Paquin? Even Veronica had heard of her, but Mrs Jenkins would not be stopped. "But surely such an eminent designer would not wish to work on *her*."

"You mean her deformed back?"

Veronica frowned; she did not like being discussed as if she were not present.

"Yes, of course, that's what I mean," hissed Mrs Jenkins.

"I believe that if Lady Katherine requests a wedding dress for her daughter-in-law to be, Madame Paquin will be happy to supply it." He took a deep breath. "I do not believe that decision is part of your remit."

Veronica was having trouble concentrating. Polly would become her Lady's maid proper, she was to have a dress designed by Jeanne Paquin—perhaps—and she would remain living here. It was like a beautiful dream.

Mrs Jenkins was now leaning forward, her face twisted and her voice getting even quieter. "Her parents do not allow her to leave the house."

"She has been sold to Lord Jameson," said Mr Slack. "They no longer have any say in the matter."

Mrs Jenkins sat back with a suddenness that rocked her chair on to its back legs.

Veronica blinked. Sold? She had been *sold*? She sat amid the ruins of her beautiful dream.

Sold?

And if she had been sold, even as Polly had said, what had been bought?

xxii

Her lesson with Mr Plumley had been delayed by the interview with Lord Jameson's secretary. Once the pleasantries had been dealt with she picked herself up and walked with as much dignity as she could muster out, across the hall and into the library.

He was waiting behind the table, while Polly stood near the window. She was holding something behind her back but Veronica was, for the moment, still thinking.

She sat down opposite Mr Plumley and stared at the table. Her back had decided to ache and she did not want to contort herself so that she was able to look him in the face.

"Why am I being married off?" she said, almost to herself though she spoke the words out loud.

"Surely that is the desire of every w-woman," said Mr Plumley.

His comment stirred something within her and her despondency coalesced into a white heat of anger. She stood up again so that she could look down on him without bending her back.

"Polly. Lock the door."

She killed the smile that had begun to emerge on Mr Plumley's face. "Get on the floor."

He pushed back his chair so quickly it wobbled as if it was going to fall. Mr Plumley disappeared beneath the table as the key clicked the lock.

"What have you got, Polly?"

"The camera, mistress."

"Good."

"Camera?" His voice wavered as it rose from the floor.

She ignored him. *The desire of every woman? Ha.*

She crossed the room to the divan. Polly ran over and arranged the cushions so they would support her back. Veronica sat and with Polly's assistance arranged herself in a reclining position. She could now see Mr Plumley still on all fours beneath the table.

Veronica pulled at her skirts until they revealed her legs to the knee. He must be slavering like one of Pavlov's dog, she thought, as she saw him wiping his mouth with the back of his hand. Salivating at the prospect of tasting her feet.

She despised him.

"Come," she said.

He was not a young man and he crawled stiffly across the carpet. But his eyes were glued to her feet. When he was a yard away she commanded him to stop and he did so.

She pulled a face, he really was drooling. A drop of saliva fell into the carpet weave darkening it with its dampness.

"Polly, remove my footwear."

"Yes, Mistress Nika."

The maid put the brown box of a camera on the end of the divan and crouched at her feet, obscuring Mr Plumley's view.

"Wait," said Veronica. "Plumley, move to there." She pointed to a position on the carpet where he would be able to see the shoes and stockings come off. If he noted the missing honorific he said nothing.

Polly removed the shoes and placed them beneath the divan, then rolled down each of her stockings. Mr Plumley was already sniffing the air as her foot odour floated across to him. Once she had finished the maid stood back and picked up the camera.

"Clean my feet, Plumley."

"Thank you, M-mistress N-nika."

He moved up and spent a few minutes sniffing, just as he had before. Then he stuck out his tongue and began his work.

As they had agreed Polly took four photographs, each one focusing on Mr Plumley's face and Veronica's feet. Not including anything that could identify her or the room.

Veronica felt her anger fading to be replaced only by boredom and the irritation of having to suppress the reaction to the tickling of his tongue.

Then he engulfed her entire big toe in his mouth, and that got her attention. It was a very interesting sensation and made the place between her legs tingle pleasantly. The warmth of his mouth, the dampness and the tongue washing along the underside, then across the top. It was delicious.

She felt a little more pleasantly disposed towards him. He did the same thing to her other big toe, which was equally stimulating. She was tempted to touch herself but felt that being aloof was more important. Besides, denying herself had its own piquant pleasure.

Finally he was done and backed away on all fours. She thought more stiffly than he had approached her. He was probably not very flexible at his age.

Polly set about drying her feet, since she had, quite sensibly, brought a hand towel with her. Then she put the stockings back on her mistress, and buckled up her shoes. Mr Plumley was looking her feet wistfully.

"You can get up now, Plumley."

"Thank you, M-mistress N-nika."

He stood up and brushed the creases from his clothes, walked to the table and sat as if nothing unusual had occurred. Polly helped Veronica off the divan and went to unlock the door.

Veronica took her place opposite Mr Plumley.

"I do not know that we will be able to continue after I am married," she said.

"I understand," he said. "I am grateful f-for the time w-we have had together. If w-we cannot continue I shall be content. B-but m-may I ask a f-favour?"

"You may ask, sir."

"M-may I have a copy of the p-p-pictures your m-maid took? It would be p-pleasant to look at them and remember how delicious your f-feet w-were."

Which reminded Veronica of the little problem she had in regard to the pictures. She had no idea how to get the images on the internal film onto photographic paper. Obviously she could not possibly give the film to someone else considering the content. She felt that telling Mr Plumley might negate the control the images gave her over him.

So she smiled. "Of course."

With that matter concluded she remembered why she had been so angry.

"Mr Plumley, as you know you were never required to teach the etiquette of society," she said. "A confusing situation has occurred and I wondered, perhaps, whether you can help me to understand it."

"I w-will endeavour to do so."

"My parents, in their wisdom—" she could not keep the sarcasm from her voice but Mr Plumley seemed not to notice, "—chose to keep me away from all decent society, and I had come to expect that I would never be married because of my ugliness and deformity."

"That is w-what one m-might expect under the circumstances."

His matter-of-factness made her anger flare up again and she had to resist the temptation to kick him under the table.

"Yes. Quite," she said. "In my meeting with Mr Slack he said I had been *sold* to Lord Jameson. I was under the impression that slavery had been outlawed, and women have achieved considerable emancipation."

"I understand your confusion, Miss Clifford-Hughes," he said. "Yes, of course, slavery is not p-practised in the British Empire and has not b-been for nearly a century. B-but until you are of age your father can dispose of you as he w-wills."

She held down her temper with difficulty. Her body so tense with the effort that her back ached terribly.

"But why?" she said. "After keeping me from society, why make me marry?"

"W-well, it is a v-very good m-marriage f-for you." Mr Plumley spoke hesitantly, as if he had no idea why she seemed to be protesting. "You are m-marrying into the aristocracy, w-which increases your rank considerably. After all your f-father's wealth comes f-from the b-businesses he created himself."

"But why would Lord Jameson agree to the match? He gains nothing from it. If I have been bought, what was the price?"

Mr Plumley shrugged. "I am afraid I am not p-privy to that information." He opened one of the text books. "I think it's w-well b-beyond time to b-begin our lessons, don't you think?"

Veronica pursed her lips and glanced out of the window. She could see Seth's head moving behind a neatly cut hedge.

She relaxed a little as she imagined touching him again, and him touching her.

She needed to study, but not boring textbooks; she needed to learn what could be done with a man's body.

And soon.

xxiii

The weather continued foul for the rest of the week. A dreary end to June and a disappointing beginning for July.

By Saturday Veronica felt as if the walls were closing in on her. An odd thing for her since she had spent so much time within them. But it seemed that this new Veronica did not like to be trapped inside the house for days on end, where the old one would have stayed in for months and not thought a thing of it.

Polly had come to her room in the morning as usual and they had brought one another to the peak of pleasure as usual. "As usual"? It was almost boring, thought Veronica. She enjoyed it, that was not the issue, but she found she wanted more.

She had her lesson with Mr Plumley. Today was not to be one for him to clean her feet because, as she pointed out, if he waited until Monday she would have had three days of feet encased in shoes so they would be particularly ripe. The prospect pleased him.

The question of developing the film continued to trouble her. She had done some research and discovered they needed a "dark room". That and some specialised equipment and chemicals, all of which could be purchased from the Kodak company. If one had access to money. She did not wish to renege on her agreement with Mr Plumley, nor did she wish to antagonise him into doing something they might both regret.

And then there was Seth and the agriculture.

After luncheon and during Polly's afternoon off, Veronica decided to go out into the garden again. All these questions were vexing her, along with the pressure of being inside against her will.

But to go out she needed to be dressed and to be dressed she needed a maid because, unlike normal women, there were some things she simply could not do for herself. So she did what for the previous incarnation of Veronica would have been unthinkable: she sought out Mrs Jenkins.

The housekeeper had her own office which was just at the top of the stairs going down to the kitchens. It was not very big but the mere fact she had a space of her own indicated her importance in the household. Mr Laughton also had an office but his was not small, though it too was out of the way. After all, he was still a servant.

She had to remind herself. They were servants and she, Veronica, was betrothed to the nobility. However, Mrs Jenkins could still make her life miserable. It would be best not to aggravate her.

So Veronica knocked but there was no reply. Mrs Jenkins was not in her room. Veronica frowned, where could she be? The answer to that was easy: she was the housekeeper, she could be anywhere in the house or out on a trip.

"Can I help you, miss?"

The butler, Emlyn Jones, stood behind her. He was tall and thin, and easily the oldest person Veronica knew. He was so tall that she was unable to raise her head sufficiently to see higher than his shoulders.

"I want to go outside and I need a maid to help me change," she said. "I hoped Mrs Jenkins could arrange it."

"Of course, miss, I believe Mrs Jenkins is in conference with the steward at this moment. If you would like to return to your room, I will find someone to assist you."

"Thank you, Jones."

And then she burst into tears. Within moments a handkerchief was being thrust gently into her hand. Her fingers brushed against his. They were cold and bony, the skin stretched tight with darker patches against the pink. The lace work of his veins were clearly visible.

"Is there something the matter, miss?"

"I don't know why I'm crying."

"I have heard the fairer sex is prone to it, miss, I wouldn't be too concerned."

She sniffed and then blew her nose. She wanted to look at his face but he was just too high. "Could you sit down, Jones?"

"That would be a terrible breach of etiquette, miss."

"Stop being so damnably proper and sit down." She waved her hand at the hardback wooden chair that sat opposite the door. Who knew why they would put one there? For people waiting to see Mrs Jenkins?

Mr Emlyn Jones stepped across to the chair and folded himself into it. He sat ramrod straight with his hands on his knees and his elbows held in. The thin face with its large nose came into view, eyes circled by wrinkles, sparse grey hair on his head.

"I just wanted to be able to look at you properly, Jones," she said.

He nodded. "I see, miss."

She wiped her eyes with the kerchief. "I know why I was crying, Jones."

"That's good, miss."

"It's because you didn't question my intentions."

"I see, miss."

"Everybody always wants to know why. Everybody always questions what I'm doing. Everybody looks down at me."

"Especially me, miss?"

Veronica frowned and then laughed through her tears. "Yes! Yes, especially you, Jones. You are far too tall."

"That's all right, miss," he said without the slightest smile. "I look down on everybody."

She giggled and then cried again. "I should have you beaten, Jones."

"Oh? Why miss, have I done something wrong?"

"Because I never knew you were funny and that you could make me laugh." She sniffed again and wiped her nose. "We could have been friends."

"I am sad that cannot happen."

"Well, since I will soon be your mistress in this house, I insist that you do become my friend."

"Sadly, miss, that would be entirely inappropriate. The lady of the house may not be friends with the staff. It makes them impossible to control. They will take advantage of your goodness and before long everything will have gone to wrack and ruin."

"Is it truly impossible?"

"It may be allowed if one is discreet," he said looking her directly in the eye. "Any carrying-on must performed out of sight and out of mind. If you understand my meaning, miss."

She hesitated, not entirely sure who he was talking about any more.

"It is easier to give oneself private moments with one's friends when they are close to you, even if they are servants. But even then one must be careful that no one hears what you are doing. There might be talk."

"You mean me and—" He held up his hand and she stopped speaking.

"I have spent many years serving this household, miss, and I have heard and seen many things. Some that I would have preferred not to see, preferred not to hear. I take my duties seriously and do not betray the trust I have been given even though it may pain me."

"When I am married your duty will be to me."

"My duty has always been to you, miss."

"Even though I am what I am?"

He smiled a sad and gentle smile. "You may be a hunchback, miss, but I am—as you pointed out—very tall. Excessively tall. Before my tenth birthday I exceeded the height of my father. I am as unnatural as you are. I am a giant."

Veronica had something in her heart that wanted to break free. Yet there were no words that would let it go. Instead she took five paces forward and threw her arms around the butler. Her heart pounded and felt as if it would explode. She cried again and sobbed into his shoulder though she was not sure whether she was crying for herself or for Emlyn Jones.

xxiv

The maid was called Elisabeth and she was not like Polly at all. The girl was clearly unhappy at having to help dress the deformed daughter of the house. She was awkward and kept mishandling the clothes that were not shaped quite the way she expected, which was upsetting for the both of them.

But, eventually, Veronica was dressed for the outside, which threatened rain at any moment from the low dark clouds that were being driven across the sky at extreme velocity.

Downstairs Elisabeth helped Veronica with her outdoor coat. She only possessed one which she used on Sundays for the walk to church during inclement weather. An umbrella was supplied and Veronica stepped out into the brisk air on her own.

Elisabeth should have come with her but Veronica did not insist on it and the girl was clearly grateful not to have to go out into the wind and rain.

Not that it was raining.

Veronica decided to take a turn around the house and see if she could see Seth. She had already decided that she would speak to him if she saw him. Etiquette be damned.

Although there was a paved walkway that circumnavigated the main building, only those parts at the back and the front were in regular use. And, in order to prevent accidental (or intentional) viewing of the owners or their guests within the house, rhododendrons and small fir trees were planted in such a way as to block the view. There was also the practical matter that gutters and sewer pipes came down the walls at intervals and their outlets were hidden from view.

However, the path went between them and the walls of the house. Once Veronica had turned the first corner as she headed in a clockwise direction, she was hidden behind summer foliage. The damp vegetation had a distinct woody smell along with the loam. Though she held her breath as she passed the sewer pipes.

Inside plumbing was quite the thing nowadays but these had only been put in relatively recently.

It was the sound of the "oh" that stopped her in her tracks. She knew that sound very well, she made it herself—as did Polly—when she was deep in the entrapment of lust.

There was a woman nearby enjoying some stimulation. Veronica felt herself getting wet as the "oh" was repeated in a regular rhythm. Veronica smiled, it was a delicious sound.

She looked around to see if she could identify the source but was confronted only by the stone walls of the house and the greenery. She took a few paces forward and the sound increased. She frowned; the sound was from above her but she was not able to tilt her head to see.

A hand came down on her shoulder and she gave a cry. The "oh"s ceased and there was whispering. Veronica turned as a hand clamped over her mouth. A rough and dirty hand. Then she saw Seth, putting his other hand to his lips and his arm around her waist, pulling her against the wall. He gesticulated upwards and then returned his finger to his mouth to indicate the need for silence.

He smelled of damp and woodsmoke.

"Nothing," said the voice of Mr Laughton from above her. "Probably a bird."

Then there was the distinct sound of a hand slapping soft flesh.

"Oh!"

Mrs Jenkins? Mr Laughton and Mrs Jenkins? Her eyes widened in astonishment, she really had never thought they had it in them. Then she imagined Mrs Jenkins jugs squashed between her body and the table top. Her naked rear—as much as Veronica could imagine it—and her delta of Venus a secret behind a dark bush, waiting for a hand to penetrate it. The "oh"s started up again, making Veronica's lust rise.

"Spyin', Miss Veronica?" said Seth. He leaned down and brought his head close to hers so that he could speak in the very quietest whisper directly into her ear. She could feel his breath brushing her skin and it made her desire rage all the more.

His ear was there. She could see the hairs of his head. The short prickly ones of his unshaven cheek and the longer ones of his side burns and the greasy mop on his head.

"I was just going for a walk," she breathed into his ear, making sure the air from her mouth went directly into his ear. She rested her cheek against his and the bristles scratched. She stuck out her tongue and licked the lobe of his ear. He breathed in sharply.

Good, let's remember who is the mistress here.

She ran her tongue along the ridges of his ear and pressed it into the hole. She pulled a face. Earwax was disgusting, but she did not let it stop her, she moved her tongue up as far as she could reach. He was like a statue, as if her actions had turned him to stone.

She pulled her head back but kept her cheek in contact. The bristles of his face scratched across her hot skin. Their noses touched and she pressed her lips against his. She breathed out long and hard through her nose and breathed in again, taking in the smell of him. She pushed his lips apart with hers and pushed her tongue into his mouth.

Then he came alive.

One arm encircled her waist and he tried to pull her towards him. Her back could not bend that way and the pain shot through. "No," she hissed, trying to make as little noise as possible. The sounds from the room did not falter. "My back."

He let her go entirely. Veronica tried to force a smile on to her face but it was not very successful. She stepped back to the wall. Seth looked forlorn, and she was glad that hurting her had that effect. She gave him an encouraging nod and reached out to take his hand in hers. With her other hand she beckoned him closer again and pulled his head down to her once more.

The one hand she placed on her waist, she found the other and pressed it to her breast. He did not move either as if he were afraid she was made from china and would shatter at his touch. "Come to me in the morning."

"I cannot enter the house, mistress."

"The window will be open for you."

"Even in the rain?"

"It will be open," she said again.

The hand on her breast tightened and even through the layers of clothing it thrilled her. The span of his palm and fingers were so much more than Polly's.

Mrs Jenkins "oh"s were being emitted at a faster rate and were now accompanied by grunts from Mr Laughton. An idea sprung into her head. "Can you lift me?"

He pulled back a little. "What do thee need?"

"I want to see them," she said and pointed up.

He looked doubtful.

"Don't you have a ladder?"

If Mrs Jenkins and Mr Laughton had been trying to be quiet before, they were not any more. They both grunted rhythmically. If Veronica couldn't get Seth to hurry it would all be over.

She hiked up her skirts revealing her legs, "Lift me" she ordered and turned to face the wall. The next thing she knew Seth's bare arms were wrapped around her calves. She went up like a firework and had to drop her dress to grab at the wall for support.

Looking down all she could see of Seth was his feet, almost as if they were her own. Her eyes were just at the level of the window ledge but to the side. She leaned sideways hoping that the two fornicators—another favourite word of the vicar that she now understood—were facing away.

They weren't but nor were they facing directly towards her. There was a desk in the window bay set at an angle. Mr Laughton was fully clothed except for his trousers and underwear which were around his ankles.

Seth shifted his weight and Veronica wobbled. She was terrified he would drop her but when he settled once more, the position seemed firmer. His breath moved against her bare thigh and she wished she had not worn any drawers.

Her eyes widened as she felt something against her other thigh. One of his hands was free to roam. She hoped it knew what it was doing, and tried to focus on the two people *fucking* in the room. She felt quite daring using the word, even if it was only in her head.

She focussed on Mr Laughton. His shirt-tail was hanging down and hid his bum, not that she was particularly interested in that portion of his anatomy.

Seth's free hand distracted her as it crept up her thigh, inside the leg of her drawers. She wouldn't have been surprised if he had walked it like a pretend spider, but he slid slowly upwards as if expecting to be told to stop at any moment. She wished she could tell him to get on with it.

Back to the window: Mrs Jenkins was almost screaming now. She was face down bent across the desk—the way her father had forced himself on Polly—her legs wide apart with her skirts thrown up across her back and her drawers around one ankle. Mr Laughton was thrusting his hips against her behind.

From what Veronica understood his prick must be inside her and he was pushing it in and out.

The thought of it made her bubbling lust come to the boil. Seth's hand had reached the top of her thigh. She dare not move in case either they fell, or even worse he thought he should stop. Right now she desperately wanted a couple of his fingers inside her—it did occur to her they would be dirty, but at this moment she really didn't care.

Mrs Jenkins was groaning at each thrust now.

Seth touched Veronica's behind. She could feel her wetness leaking down her thighs. The urge to squeeze her tits was intense but the position was far too precarious.

Mr Laughton let out a final growl-groan-yell. He stopped doing the big thrusts and just did some small ones each with a moan accompanying it. Then he withdrew. Veronica ducked her head back just as Seth gained the courage to purposefully slide his hand between her tight thighs. His fingers barely reached her secret place and she felt them catch on some of her hair.

A door slammed in the room. Veronica peeked back inside. Mr Laughton was not in sight, though she could not see the entire room. Mrs Jenkins lay there on the desk panting and whimpering. The hair around her bum and quim was matted and wet. A thick white liquid slid from her open hole, dripped down in a long strand to land on the polished wooden floor.

Mrs Jenkins' breathing was returning to normal but still she lay there. Veronica knew that she had not come, even though she must have been on the way. It was just as Polly said: men just wanted their own pleasure and had no regard for the woman's.

Veronica gave her legs a little kick and the hand withdrew from between her damp thighs. She had quite lost her desire for the moment and she was very surprised that she felt sympathy for Mrs Jenkins, a woman who had never given Veronica's happiness the slightest consideration.

Seth let her down gently. He really was very strong. He looked into her face trying to see if he had done anything wrong. She smiled and took the hand that had been jammed into her nethers and kissed the tips of the fingers where they were still sticky with her juices.

She had been right, they really were rather dirty. Good thing he had not got them inside her this time. But there was plenty of time for that.

Taking him by the hand she led him further along the path and away from the window. Once she was sure they were out of earshot, and hidden behind a mass of rhododendrons, she drew him down and kissed him again.

"I hurt thee," he said by way of apology.

"I just don't bend that way," she said.

"Thee took no offence at my liberties?"

"I enjoyed your liberties, Seth, but next time you have the opportunity to take them, your hands need to be clean. I don't want soil in my private places."

He looked mortified again, so she smiled and kissed him. Goodness, men really were such delicate things in some ways.

"The window will be open," she said, then realised tomorrow was Sunday. "On Monday."

XXV

Veronica came down early on Sunday ready for the walk to church, even though it was misty with drizzly rain. Polly had gone off to get herself ready, and probably be diddled by the mysterious Ursula. Polly enjoyed coming as much as Veronica herself, and took every opportunity, but was less interested in trying different things.

They had fallen into a routine and Polly seemed happy for it to remain the same each morning. Oh, it was true the number of fingers inserted might change, or the time spent stimulating the nubbin, whoever's it happened to be. But that was where variety ceased.

Polly was not interested in Seth, which did present Veronica with a little bit of a problem since she had not told Polly of the arrangement for Monday morning.

She was also aware of the warning from the butler about noise. Both of them liked to make a lot of noise when they were coming, just like Mrs Jenkins and Mr Laughton. When Veronica mentioned it, Polly said everybody in the household knew.

"Do they know about us?"

"Only the upstairs maids."

"Only? They'll talk," she said.

Polly shook her head. "Secrets are currency, miss. You don't squander them with idle chit-chat."

"So my life is to be traded as and when needed?"

And to that Polly had had no answer.

As she waited in the hall for Mrs Jenkins, Veronica contemplated the problem more. Or was it a problem that her activities were known? No, she thought, in the same way that she was not concerned about exposing her body, she was not concerned that others heard her moaning and crying out in lustful pleasure. That was not the problem at all. The issue was that she might be stopped.

Though it seemed as if that situation would soon be at an end as well. Once she was married she would be mistress of the house. Mrs Jenkins would no longer be able to dictate her will.

The price, unfortunately, was a husband and he remained an unknown entity.

Speak of the devil, she thought as the precise click-click of the housekeeper's heels preceded her appearance in the hall. She was as stern as ever, perhaps more so. But Veronica knew what her nether regions looked like and that certainly made the woman less frightening.

A glance at the clock showed they would need to step lively if they were to arrive on time but Mrs Jenkins seemed in no hurry.

Veronica shifted her weight from foot to foot. If they delayed she was sure to be blamed. Then she heard the carriage and turned to the door. Sure enough, through the glass, the landau with its hoods up arrived outside the front door. They were going to ride.

"Come long, Miss Clifford-Hughes," said Mrs Jameson as she breezed past her and out of the door before Veronica could say sixpence. She did not hold the door and it swung closed before Veronica reached it. Opening it was a strain. Clearly Mrs Jameson was going to make the most of the final few weeks.

The footman, one of the stablehands, put down a block for Veronica to step on to get into the carriage. The first step was far too high. She thanked him and wondered that it had happened at all. It was not as if she rode in the carriage often. Almost never. Still, she was grateful for it.

She sat down on the old leather seats that had seen better days. They were cracked in places but the smell of wax showed they had been buffed up in advance. Though covered the carriage had no windows and the rain still managed to get in. But it was better than walking.

"Are we to sit in our usual places?" asked Veronica as the carriage pulled away, bouncing deeply on its suspension.

"I think that would be best."

Yes, it probably would. Getting married was not going to change the way the rest of the village thought about her.

"Was there ever a Mr Jenkins?" she asked without thinking.

The only sounds were the wheels squelching through the mud, the damp squidge of hooves, and the birds who had not been put-off by the rain.

"There was." Mrs Jenkins words were almost a sigh and, while the house-keeper usually spoke in clipped tones, this carried the hint of an accent, though Veronica did not have the experience to know where from.

"What happened to him?"

She fully expected Mrs Jenkins to say that he had cheated on her and that she had poisoned him then buried him in the garden. But it seemed this was not a cheap tale from a cheaper story collection.

"He was a soldier. He was killed in South Africa."

"By the Boers?"

"Natives."

As far as Veronica could remember this was the longest conversation she had ever had with Mrs Jenkins. Perhaps it was not surprising since they were being forced into close proximity and did not have to concentrate on walking.

"I am sorry," said Veronica and discovered she meant it. "Do you know why I am being married to Edwin Jameson?"

"I do not."

And that was the end of that.

The carriage came out on to the road and turned in the direction of the church. It took another five minutes with the sound of bells getting louder as they travelled. Then they stopped and moments later the carriage came to a halt directly outside the door.

The block was once again put in place and the footman handed her down to the ground. There was no one about. The rest of the congregation would be inside as usual, so that they did not have to look at her.

However, looking at her was the only thing the entire collected members of the village and, it seemed, people from even further out, had any interest in do-ing. When she stepped through the entrance and into the church proper every bench was full and every face was looking at her.

It was stifling, whether it was the people, or the damp warmth of the morn-ing she did not know. But she could barely breathe and took a step back. They were like animals, waiting to pounce on her and eat her up. And the silence, not a single one of them spoke, just stared.

Even Mrs Jenkins was confused. There was no place for them to sit at the back. Every bench was filled with men, women and children.

Somewhere from the midst of the throng a small voice said, "She not look like a devil." There was a sudden in-drawing of breath as if the child had revealed the thoughts they pretended they did not have.

Is that what they really *think?* It was a moment of revelation. It was true she always pretended that they thought of her as a monster but that was to justify her keeping her distance from them. But now she knew. She really was a freak to them.

Very well, if that's what they thought then that is what she would be. She could not throw her shoulders back and stalk imposingly down the aisle but she refused to hide at the back any longer.

She walked slowly down the central aisle. She let them see her. She would even have stripped herself naked to shock them all the more, but that might stop the marriage. Because now, though she had not welcomed it, it was this betrothal that made them sit up and take notice of her.

Behind her the footsteps of Mrs Jenkins followed. The crowds still stared, but she ignored them. There was a quiet rustle of clothing as they turned to watch her as she passed. Ahead, near the altar, was the vicar, probably shocked at the size of his congregation. Behind him, in the stained-glass window, was the young St Agnes, patron saint of virgins. Veronica wondered whether having Polly's fingers inside her meant that she was still a virgin. But she did not care.

Two women slipped out the pews near the front. Polly and Ursula. As Veronica approached Polly indicated she should use the bench they had vacated. When she looked along the pew she saw the butler and in the seat behind was Seth. She allowed herself a slight smile as she slid into the gap and moved up close to Mr Jones.

After its delayed start the service went ahead as usual until the Banns were read. The announcement of her forthcoming marriage to the Honourable Edwin Jameson raised a murmur. At least among those who either could not read since the announcement had been posted in the entrance, or were deaf since the size of the crowd demonstrated the forthcoming nuptials were the talk of the area.

This was followed by a sermon on the sanctity of marriage.

Veronica listened and wondered. Her activities—what the vicar would no doubt refer to as *sordid* and not involving the production of children—of the last few weeks were certainly in contradiction to the sanctity of marriage. And therein lay a definite problem, at least for her, since she could not for one moment imagine giving them up, even if she had a husband.

He would have to lock her up and even then he could not prevent her from thinking.

She would not stop giving and receiving pleasure from Polly. She certainly needed to experiment with Seth to learn what to do with her husband, and there was Mr Plumley. He had done much to help her, and could potentially do more, so she felt almost obligated to let him lick her feet. And there was Ursula who she was very keen to get to the bottom of.

Getting to the bottom of Ursula's bottom.

She had to suppress a giggle because one never laughed in church. It was far too disrespectful. Perhaps the people were right about her, it might be that she was a devil after all.

xxvi

After church Veronica suffered the stares of the crowds. Since she was not sitting at the back she was forced to get up before the others in their pew. Rather than heading for the exit at the rear, Mrs Jenkins walked up to the front and Veronica went with her. This allowed the rest of the congregation to leave, but she was standing directly in their line of sight.

Her hump embarrassed her. The only way she could hide it was by facing them herself. Though since the natural angle of her head was down even that did not work well.

As if she understood the problem, Polly came up the aisle as well and stood an appropriate distance away, followed by the tall red-headed Ursula. The two of them blocked the view, Ursula particularly useful in that respect.

Veronica did not know what to say but she was grateful, and would have to thank Polly later. Mrs Jenkins would not consider it appropriate for her to speak to any servant under the circumstances.

The crowd filtered from the church. Polly and Ursula left the two of them alone. Finally Mrs Jenkins lead the way down the aisle and Veronica had the strangest feeling she was seeing the church as she would on the day of her wedding. Empty.

The periodicals she read would sometimes show artists' illustrations, and even photographs, of the gaudy affairs in London. The coronation of George IV after his father's short reign had been widely photographed and recorded in journals and magazines. There were always crowds but there would be no crowds for her.

She and Mrs Jenkins did not speak on the return journey. Veronica felt sad though she did not know why.

When they reached the house and were divesting themselves of their coats, Veronica said: "I will take luncheon in my room, Mrs Jenkins."

Mrs Jenkins hesitated as if she intended to object and then almost appeared to deflate. "Yes, Miss Clifford-Hughes."

And that was that. It seemed her position in the house had changed.

Veronica climbed the stairs slowly. The carriage was no less irksome to her back than simply walking. She needed to rest and when she reached her room she lay down on the bed, on her side as usual and her head propped up on a pillow so her neck was straight.

She dozed and was woken by Polly coming in with her luncheon. The maid placed the tray on the small table and then set about removing Veronica's shoes.

"You've got dirt on the counterpane."

"Yes," said Veronica. "It's wet out."

"You certainly caused a stir." Polly rolled down Veronica's stockings taking a moment to reach further up her dress than was entirely necessary and stroke her mistress's thighs.

Veronica appreciated the thought but on this occasion chose not to react.

"Do you want to get out of your dress?" asked Polly as she stowed the shoes and deposited the stockings in the laundry basket. "There's mud on the hem."

Veronica pushed herself to the edge of the bed and sat up. She noted that the door was still unbolted then stood up.

"Later," she said, glanced at Polly and taking a deep breath. "There are one or two things we must discuss."

Polly's reaction was to go completely still, like a deer you might stumble across in the woods before it disappears into the trees in fear.

"Let's sit," said Veronica, indicating the armchair that was easily big enough to accommodate them both, crushed together so touching was inescapable. Polly went to the door instead and applied the lower bolt.

She returned and placed the cushions for Veronica, who sat hard over on one side to make as much room as possible for the maid. Polly did not seem enthusiastic as she sat. Certainly not as happy as when she joined her mistress in bed.

"I have good news, and other news," said Veronica. She imagined she might even be able to feel Polly's heart beat faster.

"Not bad news?"

"I don't think so and I don't want you to think it so either."

"Tell me the good news."

"Lord Jameson's family has agreed I must have a Lady's maid, and I said it must be you."

Polly was silent. Veronica shifted in the chair so she was turned more to face the maid. Her face was in profile just inches from Veronica, who could smell the girl's lavender scent.

Veronica put her hand on Polly's. "Isn't that good news?"

Polly turned her face to Veronica. "It is lovely news, Nika."

But Veronica frowned. "You're not happy about it."

Polly kissed her on the nose since it was in such easy reach. "No, I am pleased, of course I am. It's wonderful news, the extra money will be useful and we can be close all the time. And Mrs Jenkins won't be able to dictate to me."

"But?"

"I won't have Ursula."

Veronica was annoyed. And knew she did not really have the right. Even so, who was Ursula? But Polly liked her—no, Polly liked what Ursula did to her without demanding anything in return. It was selfish.

But then wasn't Veronica herself selfish too? She wanted Polly for herself but then she wanted everyone else too.

"What's the not-truly-bad news?" asked Polly, interrupting Veronica's train of thought.

It was Veronica's turn to be silent.

"What's wrong?"

"Nothing, nothing's wrong, except I am selfish."

"I don't understand."

Veronica took a deep breath. "I have invited Seth tomorrow morning."

"Oh."

"It's not because I don't want you. That's what I mean, I am greedy and selfish. And," she said, "I need to learn about male anatomy so I can please my husband."

"Are you going to let him fuck you?"

"No."

"How will you stop him? I told you what men are like."

And I have seen it with my own eyes.

"Because I want you to be there too. Together we could overpower him if we need to."

"I am not interested in his equipment."

"You don't have to be," said Veronica. "You'll be my bodyguard."

Polly laughed. "Bodyguard, what a notion."

But Veronica was serious. "From what you've told me, and what I've seen, men are very single-minded. If he gets uppity you can hit him over the head with something heavy."

Polly laughed even more.

"Why are you laughing?"

But it was impossible for Veronica to get any sense out of her maid for several minutes because as soon as the laughs began to dry up she would just start again. Eventually Veronica could not help but join in, even though she had no idea what she was laughing about.

"Will you do it?" asked Veronica when she finally got control of herself.

"Of course, I will."

"Good, in that case, Polly, I wish to be naked."

"What about me?"

"I don't know, do you wish me to be naked as well?"

"What? No."

"You don't want me naked? I am insulted."

"No, I meant should I be naked as well?"

"If you would do me the honour then yes, because I would very much like to diddle you until you scream. Then I shall diddle myself and you can watch."

"Yes, Mistress Nika."

"Any more of that, Polly, and I will order you to lick my feet clean."

And they both laughed as if they were intoxicated.

xxvii

The weather cleared up in the evening and the sun went down in a blaze of red, which was a good omen for the following day. The temperature dropped to what seemed to be very cold, though it was still the height of summer.

Veronica had gone to bed early and needed more than just a sheet to keep her warm. Lying in her usual position, she ran her hands over her breasts and scratched at her nipples through the cloth of her nightdress. As the electrifying sensations ran through her, she groaned with the pleasure of it.

She lay on her left side and kept her left hand on her breast to squeeze and scratch. With her other, she rucked up her nightdress, ran her nails through the dense dark hair between her legs and slipped her fingers between her thighs.

The folds of skin were already becoming moist and she smiled. She rubbed herself gently. The afternoon had been full of wildness as she and Polly pleasured one another, but now she felt the need for gentleness. She reached further and dipped a finger into her hole. Then slid her finger up past her peeing hole, which she had discovered with the mirror, to the nubbin which had been terribly used by Polly.

It was true that Veronica liked it when Polly roughly squeezed and twisted her nipples or her nubbin. But in her enthusiasm she did it too much, there came a point where it no longer had the desired effect, and all Veronica ended up with were bruised parts that ached.

Not that they didn't still react. They were as dedicated to lust as Veronica herself. It was odd to think of the parts of her body as separate from herself, but she did.

As the pleasures flowed through her, she fell asleep.

A tapping on the window broke into her dreams and shattered them. The sky was shining blue and the sun shone on the hills.

The tapping came again and Veronica took a moment to realise and remember that the silhouetted shape behind the glass was the under-gardener, here at her behest.

She climbed out on to the floor and fetched the chair so she could unlock the window.

She looked through the glass. He had stopped tapping and was clinging to the ivy and the window frame. There was a presumptuous grin on his face.

So she turned her back on him and walked a few steps away. Placing her feet a foot apart to steady herself she pushed first one shoulder of the nightdress to her upper arm revealing the curve of her shoulder, and then she did the same to the other.

Just as she had that morning of her birthday when things had changed, she pulled the nightdress down across her body. Inch by inch revealing her hump to him.

Let's see if he can truly bear to see it, she thought to herself. Exposing her hump was, for her, far more daring than revealing her behind, her breasts, or even her quim. She let the nightdress settle at her waist and moved gently to-and-fro as if there were music.

She pulled her arms from the nightdress but still held it up. She was now naked from the waist up. Still moving with the slow rhythm she turned round. As she faced him, not looking up, she squeezed each breast once making the nipple protrude even further.

The music in her head continued and she turned her back to him again. Let him see her hump in all its glory and horror.

Finally she pushed the nightdress from her hips and let it drop. Her bum was now revealed and he could probably see the outer lips and her hair. Veronica had come to the conclusion that this was far more alluring than the front because that was hidden behind her dark mat. It wasn't the same for Polly since her hair was so sparse and light you could see her lips clearly from the front as well.

There was a gentle knock and the door opened. Polly walked in.

"You started without me," she said with a smile. She bolted the door and turned back. "Are you going to let him in?"

"I was going to," said Veronica. "But why don't I stay here while you do it?"

"So I'm to be your pimp and you're my doxy?"

Veronica swayed to the music only she could hear. "I have no idea what you're talking about."

"I'll explain later."

Veronica heard the chair scrape and then the sound of the window being slid upwards. Two boots landed on the floor."

"Take those off right now," said Polly. "Then go and wash your hands. Did you have a bath?"

"Had a bath yesterday like the mistress said," said Seth. Veronica couldn't see him but she imagined him devouring her body with his eyes. He hadn't run scared so her hump could not be a problem.

Moments later the boots landed on the floor again and shortly thereafter there was splashing in the water bowl.

Oh dear lord, she needed to pee. If things became particularly exciting there would be no way she could control herself. Well, if it needed to be done why not make a spectacle of it?

"Polly, fetch my chamber pot please."

"Mistress?"

"If you please, and a cloth."

Veronica made sure she kept her back to Seth, she was not sure she wanted to see the look on his face. But the truth, revealed to her once again, was that she had no shame, and peeing in front of a man she barely knew did not engender any embarrassment in her.

Polly did as she was told, though, and, as she brought it while hidden from Seth's view by Veronica's naked body, she pulled a *what are you doing?* face. Veronica gave the tiniest shrug and opened her legs so Polly could place the flower-decorated ceramic bowl between them.

Using the bed to support herself, Veronica squatted over the pot and relaxed her muscles. The noise of her pee streaming into the pot seemed very loud. She kept it going for as long as she could so that she would not be distracted later. She wondered whether there might be men who would take special pleasure at this—just as Mr Plumley worshipped unclean feet—and why just men? Perhaps women too.

Polly handed her the cloth once she had finished and Veronica wiped between her legs. Polly removed the pot and its acrid smell. Veronica stretched as much as her back allowed and turned to face Seth.

The look of astonishment on his face was worth the act of peeing in front of him. Though she did not think he particularly liked it. Just that he had not expected to see the future lady of the house doing it. Veronica felt that keeping him off-balance would be the best way to approach matters. Though she had no idea what else she might do. Defecate?

Perhaps she'd keep that as a last resort. A very last resort.

"Come here, Seth."

He touched his forelock and, in his socks—which had holes in them—he walked over. His feet smelled. She wondered in passing if Mr Plumley had ever tried male feet. Did the sex of the owner matter? After all, everybody had feet.

His eyes were riveted to her breasts. Her nipples were erect and the dark skin around them was crinkled.

She wasn't sure how educated he might be in dealing with a woman's body—not that she was very experienced herself, but at least she had one and had the opportunity to experiment with Polly's. This was very difficult, certainly more difficult than she expected.

Polly came and sat in the armchair; from somewhere she had found a walking stick. Veronica smiled, which Seth assumed was for him and so he smiled as well.

"Perhaps you should remove your clothes, Seth."

"Aye, Miss Veronica."

"When we are together like this," said Veronica, "you should call me Mistress Nika."

"Miss?"

Veronica frowned. "You will call me Mistress Nika! Now take your clothes off. I want to see your body."

In quiet moments Veronica had imagined taking Seth as her lover and running away with him. But now she wasn't so sure.

xxviii

Veronica could hardly believe it. After everything Polly had said about the way men behaved: Seth was shy.

"Thee going to watch I?" he said, in his quaint dialect.

"Yes."

He hesitated. "That bain't how it be."

"That's how I want it, Seth."

And still he didn't remove his clothes. Veronica frowned. Time was getting on. How long before he would be unable to climb down the wall without being noticed?

"You didn't mind watching me take my clothes off," she said. "I think you could do me the same honour."

She knew her logic was irrefutable. And he did not attempt to refute it. He just didn't take off his clothes. Well, if that's the way he was going to be she needed to take matters into her own hands.

She stepped up to him. He was taller than her and would have been even if she wasn't forced to stoop. He was wearing a jacket so she took hold of the shoulders and pushed it back as best she could. He lifted his arms and the jacket fell from his back. It thumped as it hit the ground. He probably had gardening tools in the pockets.

His shirt was tucked into his trousers. She pulled it up at the front and then reached around to do the same at the back. This brought her breasts, upper body and cheek in contact with his torso. The feeling was so different to touching Polly: she was soft while Seth was hard.

She breathed in through her nose and smelled his earthiness. Which was probably due to the fact that his shirt had seen better days and had ingrained soil. But never mind that, it still smelled good.

Her hump was slightly more on the right than the left but it was his right hand that came down on the bare skin of her shoulder. Another difference to Polly, his hands were rough instead of smooth. The thought of them grasping and squeezing her breasts was a delight she looked forward to.

She remembered what she was supposed to be doing and pulled up the shirt at the back until it came free. She took a step back and started to tackle the buttons down the front. In one swift movement he pulled it up and off. He threw it behind him and her face was inches from the bare skin of his chest. It was very hairy and while his skin was dark the hairs were bleached pale by the sun, like that on his head. His hand returned to her shoulder and the other encircled her upper right arm.

She desperately wanted to be able to look up at him. In the stories the woman would look up into the eyes of her lover and he would stoop down and kiss her sweetly on the lips. But she was unable to look up. He kissed the top of her head. She leaned forward and kissed his chest.

His hands went to his trousers.

"Wait," she said.

"Thee wanted to see," he said with almost an accusing tone. She really was not happy with his attitude. She took a couple of steps back so that she could look him in the face.

"You will address me as Mistress Nika," she said again.

He just looked at her, his hands still on his belt buckle.

"Say it."

"Mistress Nika."

She smiled at him as his reward and he seemed to relax a little, then reached out and put her hand on his hairy forearm. "I do want to see, Seth, but I need time to examine what you have revealed to me now."

"Thee bain't no doctor."

She pulled his hand free of his belt and brought it to her. Taking it in both hands, it was almost twice the breadth of her own, she lifted it to her mouth and kissed the end of each finger. And at each kiss she opened her mouth and touched her tongue to the tip. He was transfixed. When she reached the thumb she engulfed it with her mouth.

Perhaps Mr Plumley was good for teaching her about lust too, she thought, if it hadn't had been for him she wouldn't have tried such a thing. Though there was no way in God's green earth she was going to lick Seth's feet, even if he begged her to.

She glanced across at Polly, who had an odd look on her face. Veronica was unsure whether it was surprise, jealousy, or just lust. Well that was not Veronica's problem. Right now she had Seth's body to investigate, and make him enjoy it at the same time. What did men like?

She knew what she liked and there was Seth's upper torso. She moved his hand so it rested on her shoulder—he regained control and curled the fingers round, digging into her skin. She moved forward again and laid her right hand on his chest with the left on his hip.

Absorbing the sensations in her hand she ran her fingers across his skin. She could not see his ribs where they were hidden by a thick layer of muscle. Where a woman was soft, he was muscled. She brought her hand to his nipple. It was rock hard but when she touched it he jumped.

"What thee about … Mistress Nika? Tha's not a place to touch on a man."

She was too close to look up at him. Instead she slipped her arm around his waist to pull him closer. Starting low with the other hand she brought it up towards the nipple again. He was like a nervous cat, wondering what she was going to do to him next. Pulling tighter she brought her cheek against his chest. She kissed his skin and licked him—he was salty—leaving a little moist patch. She moved a little and did it again. It calmed him. And then she brought her lips together over his nipple and then sucked and licked it.

He shivered but did not protest this time. She licked all around it and sucked again. She brought her free hand up to his other nipple and took it between her finger and thumb. As she sucked the one she rolled the other. They were both as hard and as big as hers became.

So, that was a thing learnt. Her own breasts were pressed against him and she enjoyed the pulses of pleasure from them. While his one hand was still on her shoulder, the other was doing nothing. She thought she knew why: it was that to hold her he would have to touch her hump and whether it was disgust or uncertainty about hurting her, he was avoiding doing that. In some ways she appreciated it.

She nipped his skin with her teeth and slid under his arm. The hair in his armpit was dark and had a strong, not unpleasant scent. She scraped her breasts against his body as she moved around him until directly behind and his back towered above her. He started to move.

"Stay still," she said, then changed her mind. "No, kneel down."

"Aye, Mistress Nika."

Moments later she could see his head and all of his back. The muscles around the shoulders, the shoulder blades and his beautifully straight spine. She had a moment of envy then pushed it aside. Everyone had a straight back except her—and the other hunchbacks in the world. She was alive and she was not unhappy, and she had this man doing everything she commanded.

She ran her hand across his skin pressing into the muscles and feeling the bones. The spine with its individual vertebrae. She sighed. The nature of her deformity was such that she had studied backs. She knew exactly how the perfect ones should be. She knew what hers was like. Seth's back was like a Greek god's—there were enough of them in statue form for her to know.

"Stand."

Smoothly he was on his feet again. She pressed herself against his back with her arms locked around him. Feeling her way she found his nipples once more and scratched across them, feeling him shudder, but he did not complain. Perhaps he had learnt something as well.

One hand following the other down his front she felt her way to his belt but she could not reach all the way around him. She stopped trying and moved back a little.

"Undo your belt and any other fastening," she said. As his hands went to work at the front she took hold of the belt at the sides because she wanted this to be under her control.

"Undone, Mistress Nika." He was saying her wanton name in a more relaxed way with each utterance.

She let down the trousers slowly. His hips came into view. Soft skin without any hair tight over the bone. Then his buttocks, he was not wearing any sort of drawers, and his rear was terribly hairy. But even if she had not seen a man's posterior before, she had seen Polly's and Mrs Jenkins'. There was no real difference, although his skin was tanned above the waist and still pink below it.

The thighs became exposed. The back of the knees and then she could not easily bend any further and just let the trousers fall the rest of the way. She looked back at Polly and grinned. Her maid still had the enigmatic expression on her face.

"Do not move, Seth."

"No, Mistress Nika."

Veronica stepped around him but kept her eyes away from him until she was standing directly in front of him and a short distance away. She looked into his eyes which, she noted, were once again on her breasts. *Was that all he could think of?*

Taking care to control herself she purposefully ran her eyes down his front naming the parts as they came into view until finally:

Not what she was expecting.

xxix

He had a mat of black hair in his groin, in the same way that she did. Protruding from that mass was a roll of skin. Never having seen a man's prick before—Mr Laughton had not turned in her direction after removing his from Mrs Jenkins—it was difficult for her to understand what she was looking at.

Seth adjusted his position, pulling one leg from the trousers around his ankle and placing it further out. Then he put his hands on his hips, as if he were proud of what he was showing her. Perhaps he had a right to do that, she had no idea since she had no point of reference.

What she did notice was that the socks, still on his feet, could do with darning. It was slightly comical but she suspected that laughing might not be the right thing to do at this juncture.

And then it moved. On its own. It twitched. She could only assume that it must possess its own musculature. The muscles between her own legs seemed to do very little except tighten her holes—though that could be rather pleasant if done at the right time.

Had Polly said something about it getting bigger? This one was about the length of her own hand and pointed at an angle towards the ground.

She looked him in the eye. "Do not move, Seth."

"Not move?"

"Did you not enjoy what I have done so far?"

"Aye, 'appen I have."

"Well, I wish to examine your body in more detail."

His John Thomas definitely twitched at that. "Aye, Miss Nika."

She drew closer and knelt so that her face was barely six inches from this interesting roll of skin. She could see the veins on it through what seemed to be a thick outer layer. It was an even thickness along the main length which, now she looked closer, was not straight but curved slightly to the left. The end was bulbous and an envelope of skin wrapped around it and formed a little tube at the end so that she could not see what was within. Its end looked damp. But this was not the thick white liquid—Mr Laughtons's seed—that had dripped from Mrs Jenkins quim, it was clear.

Up close she could see that there was a bag of skin that hung from the base with the shape of two balls inside it.

Men's arrangements were certainly complex.

"I am going to touch you now."

"Aye."

She was not sure but she thought perhaps his voice sounded a little strained. She looked up at Polly, still sitting in the chair, still holding the walking stick across her knees. Veronica was now certain Polly was horrified at what she was about to do. But Seth was being very obedient so Veronica was wary but not overly concerned.

Since saying she was going to touch it, it had very definitely increased in length. Not only that but its angle had decreased, such that the tip was rising up. If she was not careful it would touch her face. She sat back on her heels to give it more room.

It occurred to her that she had no idea how to touch it and she did not want to hurt him. The memory of what Polly had done to her flashed through her mind. No, she did not want to hurt him.

She could not look up at him so stared resolutely at his prick.

"Do you pleasure yourself?" she said.

There was a reluctant grunt that she took for assent.

"Show me."

"But..."

"I want to know how you do it so I can do it properly."

"It bain't proper, Mistress Nika."

"And it's proper for you to climb in through my window? Is it proper for you to see me naked? And is it proper for you to stand there and let me disrobe you so that you also stand naked?"

"No, Mistress Nika."

"Then show me, whether it's proper to do so or not."

After a pause. "Aye, Mistress Nika."

His right hand descended into her field of view and wrapped around the flesh of his prick close to the tip. She doubted she would be able to get one of her hands all the way around it. Still gripping he pulled in towards his body. It seemed the skin was loose and could move easily, and as he did so the bulbous end came into view. Purplish in colour, the skin was smooth, and shiny with a slick wetness.

He pulled all the way back until his hand was pressed against his body. Then he moved it forwards again all the way to the tip. The act of doing this must have stimulated him because his prick thickened even more, lengthened and, by the time, he was going back on the second stroke his prick was pointed upwards.

"Let go," she ordered.

He released the flesh and it remained with the end pointing upwards. The skin did not try to move forward and cover the tip so the head of it stood free with its hole at the end from which he pissed and where his seed emerged. She frowned slightly, it was a curious economy of design. She preferred the female arrangement where the exits were separate. Still, God in his wisdom had chosen to do it that way. Or Mr Darwin was correct and it simply happened that way because it worked. Or perhaps both.

"Remarkable," she said. "Let me try."

He said nothing and she suspected he was very keen for her to do so. She realised she was very wet between her legs. It seemed her body knew exactly what this was and was readying itself, even if she had no real idea what she was doing.

She reached up and wrapped her fist around the thick roll of flesh. It was hot and the texture of the skin was soft and pliable. Yet when she squeezed—Seth groaned—it was hard beneath. She brought up her other hand so that she could encircle it. And then, slowly, carefully she pushed her hands along the shaft dragging the skin back just as he had done. Behind the head it tightened and she could have sworn that it grew in size even more. She had no idea how something so large could penetrate a woman's hole without causing pain. She was satisfied with just a couple of Polly's fingers.

Her hands came to rest in the thick hair at the base. So she reversed direction and moved her hands back towards the tip. She kept going until the skin covered the tip. Seth groaned again. She felt quite pleased, this all seemed to be going quite well. And, in a moment of revelation, she remembered the movements of Mr Laughton's behind when he was fucking the housekeeper. He had thrust in and out. So her hands were mimicking that action. Mr Laughton had moved quickly so she could undoubtedly increase the rate of strokes.

The thought was as good as the action and she stroked her hands back and forth along the length.

"Oh my lord," said Seth under his breath. His hips thrust in time with her hand movements, he was moving faster so she did as well. That was entirely natural since the same thing happened when she was diddling herself or Polly. As they were coming they went faster.

That meant he would come. Polly said men took less time.

Veronica wished she had three hands so she could rub between her legs as she stroked Seth's prick. Or four hands so she could do that and squeeze her breasts as well.

If only Polly would come over and shove her fingers into Veronica's hole. She was feeling desperate. She kept at Seth's prick even though her arms were aching and her back was straining. Seth was grunting rhythmically, not unlike Mr Laughton when he was due to come.

Veronica wanted to make Seth come. She wanted to come herself. She beat at his prick again and again. He thrust at her, the tip of his prick so close she could have licked it. Why not?

The next time she pushed back against his body she licked the end of his prick.

Seth said something guttural that she did not understand. The liquid from his prick was salty but not unpleasant. She was sure it wasn't any sort of piss. Pull back. Thrust forward. Lick the end. Again. And again. And again. She was reaching a point of exhaustion where she would not be able to continue.

She pushed. He thrust forward, she opened her mouth to lick and he groaned long. She felt muscular spasms in the base of his prick. A white liquid erupted from the end in a pulse. The first outpouring of ejaculate covered her face. She turned away and the next quantity went into her hair and her ear.

His seed erupted half a dozen times more and her face was covered. She did not care. She had done it, and she was desperate to come herself. She let him go and let herself roll over on to the floor. With her fingers slamming into her soaking cunt and the other hand crushing her own tit, she rubbed and squeezed and came as if the world was ending.

But it was not enough. She dug her nails hard into her tits and rubbed her nubbin so hard it was almost as if she would pull it from its root. She came again. And again.

She did not scream, she whimpered.

Finally too exhausted to make her muscles obey her, she went limp and fainted.

XXX

She returned to her senses and opened her eyes to find Polly wiping Seth's seed from her face with a cloth that she kept rinsing in the bowl. She was still lying where she had fallen on the floor.

"Are you all right, mistress?"

Polly seemed very concerned. Veronica took stock of herself. She ached almost everywhere. Her arms and back where she had been working on Seth; her knees and ankles because she had been kneeling all the while; and her tits and nubbin where she had abused herself so violently.

"Help me sit on the bed," she said and, with Polly's assistance, she got to her feet and the dropped on to the edge of the bed. She was sticky and Seth's seed started to drip on to her breasts. Polly cleaned her up.

"You'll have to have your hair washed, Nika."

"He certainly made a lot of seed," said Veronica. "You didn't say anything about how much they produce." Then she looked around. "Where's he gone?"

Polly nodded at the window. "He was worried when he found out the time. Scared he'd be seen climbing down, or people might wonder where he had got to."

"Did you know they produced so much?"

Polly shook her head. "I only know what went inside me."

"Do you think Seth enjoyed it?"

Her maid laughed at that. "He tried to be concerned when you fainted, but you had discombobulated him. He could barely fasten his buttons and I swear he nearly broke his neck climbing down the ivy."

"His thing seemed huge."

Polly nodded and Veronica wondered if she'd be able to persuade Polly to try Seth. Perhaps if they did it together. Or maybe if Veronica dealt with Seth and Polly just diddled Veronica. That could work.

"You get back into bed," said Polly. "I'll get a bath sorted out and we can wash your hair."

"Do I need a bath?"

136

"You stink of his seed, and your come," said Polly.

Veronica gave a little smile and slid back into the bed. Polly covered her up and gave her a kiss on the lips which involved some tongue duelling.

"You could come to bed too," said Veronica, finding her lust rising once more.

"There's no time for that and Nika, like I said, you smell and I don't want his seed on me."

She left and Veronica snuggled down even though she wasn't cold. She smiled to herself. The kiss showed Polly had become stimulated watching what Veronica had been doing to Seth. She was just pretending she hadn't.

It occurred to Veronica that if she caught Seth's emissions in her mouth it would stop him from making such a mess. She found some strands of hair that had his congealed seed in them and sucked at it. The taste wasn't delightful but it was tolerable. Cod liver oil tasted worse.

She would have to try that next time, as long as she did not get too carried away and forget.

———⬥———

"THE FACILITIES HERE are quite archaic," said her husband-to-be, the Honourable Edwin Jameson.

Her lessons had once again been interrupted, this time causing a kerfuffle. Mr Plumley had been savouring the taint of her left big toe when they heard someone at the door. Poor Mr Plumley was quite put out, though it was not he who had to out on his stockings and shoes so swiftly.

Mrs Jenkins had looked at them askance when she had been denied entry by the locked door. In fact, if Veronica was not mistaken she had sniffed the air—perhaps to determine whether there had been inappropriate goings-on. The most she would have smelled is Veronica's feet which were now damp inside her shoes.

Veronica had no time to dress more correctly for a visit and was dragged out to escort her betrothed around the property. But Edwin, as she resolved to think of him, was dressed in brown tweed which was serviceable, of highest quality, but not dressed up

At a loss to know exactly how she should behave when meeting with her future husband who she had never even had a conversation with—she was finding etiquette to be a far more important subject then she ever could have imagined—she held out her hand to him. He took it lightly in his thin, long and cold fingers and gave a little bow.

She was then introduced to a fellow who could be no more than twenty years, by the name of Lawrence Slack the Younger, who certainly resembled his father and was clearly destined to inherit the family business.

Which was the point Edwin glanced around and said, "The facilities here are quite archaic."

Mrs Jenkins was not in Edwin's sight and Veronica recognised the look of explosive anger. It would do the housekeeper's health no good at all if she had to suppress that level of antagonism for any length of time. She would probably get the vapours.

"Do you think so?" said Veronica. "In what way?"

"You have no electricity."

Veronica's heart soared. "No, indeed we do not. We do not even have gas since we are too far from a storage unit."

"Your father could have had one put in."

Veronica went cold again. She had no desire to defend her parents and their lack of attention. She thought quickly. "What would you say are the primary benefits of electricity in a private house such as this?"

"Obviously lighting which is particular benefit in the winter months. Candles can start fires."

She expected him to continue but he didn't. Instead he turned to Slack the Younger. "Make a note to have the house surveyed for electricity. We must have a generator running before the wedding and lights installed in all the main rooms, we shall decide which as we proceed."

Slack the Younger made a note.

"Now," he said, turning back to Veronica. "If you would be kind enough to show me around. We can determine which rooms will benefit most from electricity, and see what else is missing that I cannot do without."

Mrs Jenkins cleared her throat. "I would be happy to show you around, sir."

He looked at her as if she were a specimen in a display. "That will not be necessary."

And that was that.

Thankfully he did not seem to object to Polly accompanying them or, if he did, he said nothing.

They made a tour of the ground floor rooms. Veronica half-expected him to criticise them for their size, since he must be used to more and bigger ones. But he did not. The library in particular attracted his attention and he went to the trouble of pacing the dimensions. Then he sat at her father's desk; the window faced north and the light came over the shoulder on to the desk. He nodded. "An excellent arrangement."

Having returned to the hall with its tightly swept staircase up to the next level, they headed up.

"I am not sure how I should address you, Mr Jameson," said Veronica. The question had been vexing her every time she was required to speak to him.

He stopped on the stair. "An interesting question that encompasses so much history," he said.

She almost wished she had not asked, for he did seem fond of his own voice.

"However, in light of our forthcoming nuptials, I believe Edwin will be quite sufficient," he said. "Shall I call you Veronica?"

You'll be the only person who does, she thought. "That would be entirely satisfactory... Edwin."

He nodded and continued up the stairs. He was odd, she thought, but not unpleasant. Perhaps being married to him would not be so bad, and if she could do to him what she had done to Seth earlier he might even come to like her. His gaze did not linger on her hump the way most people's did, which was refreshing.

She hesitated when they came to her parents' bedroom. She could not remember the last time she had entered it. In fact the more she thought, the more certain she became that she never had. Except perhaps she had come into this world in this room. She realised she didn't even know where she had been born.

Edwin tried the handle but the door was locked.

Polly was sent off to fetch the keys, though she would probably return with Mrs Jenkins.

In the meantime Edwin wandered to the window at the end of the corridor. The day was bright but not too hot. Veronica came up beside him.

"I'm afraid our gardens will be no match for those at Launceston House."

"I care little for floral ornamentation," he said. "However, I am concerned about your vegetable garden. Is it extensive?"

"It satisfies the household to my knowledge, but I take no part in the running of the household."

"That will change."

"Of course." And the thought terrified her.

"It probably isn't enough," he said peering intently through the glass, though there was nothing but floral ornamentation to be seen.

"Enough for what?"

Abruptly he pulled back from the window and stood up straight. Unfortunately he was so close to her it took his head out of her field of vision.

"I am a member of the Vegetarian Society," he said. "Unless we are entertaining and it cannot be avoided, there will be no cooking of red meat in this house from the day we are married. And I assure you, Veronica, I do not intend to entertain any *blood-lappers*."

"Oh." She could not think of anything else to say.

No more stews? Steak? Lamb? Venison? *No more bacon?* It was little wonder no one would marry him and, as a result, she had been lumbered. After all, she was nothing.

"Yes, once you have rid your body of the poison of red meat you will soon discover the benefits. Health and life will be returned to you."

I am perfectly happy the way I am, she screamed at him in her mind but he didn't hear her. She saw him glance towards her right shoulder and she thought he might even claim that a vegetarian diet would cure her back of its curvature. If he thought it he kept it to himself, which was just as well as she felt that striking him might get their marriage off on the wrong foot.

Thankfully Polly returned with Mrs Jenkins.

xxxi

There was a musty smell to her parent's bedroom. The room was cleaned every two months just to remove the layers of dust in case the owners returned. If Veronica was expecting to find something revealing she was mistaken. It was just a room with a bed and bedroom furniture.

Edwin did not open the drawers but he checked the doors off to find the various dressing areas and a private bathroom. Veronica was astonished at the opulence of it since so little had been spent on her and the rest of the house. Perhaps it was the previous owner's doing.

But Edwin was frowning. "There are not separate bedrooms."

"Mr and Mrs Clifford-Hughes did not require a separate bedroom, sir," said Mrs Jenkins.

Veronica was lost. Why would a married couple have separate bedrooms?

"Make a note, Slack," said Edwin. "See if there's a wall to an adjoining bedroom that could be given a door."

Veronica wanted to ask whether he was planning to have this room while she had another, or the other way around, or perhaps that they would alternate. And if they were to be in separate bedrooms how would the fucking happen?

It was all very strange.

"I am quite fatigued," said Veronica. "I wonder if I might be excused the rest of the tour. Mrs Jenkins has the keys which you may need again."

Edwin was examining the bed and waved a hand in her direction.

She took it for a dismissal and left with Polly in tow. Rather than go to her bedroom, which had not yet been visited on the tour, she returned to where she had left Mr Plumley. After all that walking her feet would be ripe again and he could have at them. She did find his attentions quite relaxing. Unfortunately he had departed, and she hoped he was not too upset.

While she and Polly waited in the library for the tour to be completed, Veronica related the information about the vegetarianism. Polly's eyes went wide. "Cook will have an apoplectic! The men won't stand for it."

"What can they do?"

"Find another position," said Polly seriously.

"But won't that be hard?"

Polly shook her head. "Not if it happens to be mentioned they were driven away by the quality of food. Or lack of it."

"Oh dear," said Veronica. "And I have to run the household. I have no idea what I must do."

"There are books. Mrs Beeton's Household Management."

"More studying."

———◉———

EVENTUALLY EDWIN AND his man left having been through the servants quarters in the top two floors and then below stairs. Veronica saw him off at the door and this time he actually touched his lips to her hand. They were cold too. If that was the result of being a vegetarian, she wanted nothing to do with it.

"I will return to examine the vegetable garden," he said as his parting shot.

"Lovely," said Veronica and waved as he climbed into the back of a steam landau with his family crest on the side.

She turned to face Mrs Jenkins who stood behind her. For once they seemed to have a kind of sisterliness as they had both suffered at the hands of this strange man.

"You are going to London tomorrow," said the housekeeper. "To be measured and fitted for your dress."

"This is none of my doing, Mrs Jenkins." Veronica did not know why she was apologising, since it was not as if she truly cared what the woman thought. "I would just as soon stay a spinster the rest of my life."

"If wishes were horses, beggars would ride."

Veronica frowned. "Yes."

Mrs Jenkins took a deep breath. "Please come into the library, there is something we need to discuss."

"Wait here, Polly."

"No, she must come as well."

Veronica felt the coldness of discovered guilt creeping through her. Did Mrs Jenkins know what they did of a morning? And afternoon, and evening if possible. Had Seth been spotted climbing from her window that morning?

Or the other morning. Had she been seen exposing herself at the window? Did Mrs Jenkins know what Mr Plumley did?

Veronica glanced at Polly who was looking equally guilty.

They went in. Mrs Jenkins closed the door but did not lock it. She indicated for Veronica to sit by the table as she did herself. Polly remained standing.

Mrs Jenkins cleared her throat. "You are not experienced in the outside world."

Veronica did not think that needed any response. The furthest she had been was the village.

"Do you know what to do if you are caught short on the train? In a shop? Or someone's house?"

"Ask where the W.C. is?"

Mrs Jenkins shook her head. "You do not get caught short anywhere."

Veronica stared at her, then glanced at Polly who looked equally perplexed. "I don't think that's possible."

"Not without help, and that is why I am discussing this. In the first instance you must reduce how much you drink from now. And be sure to empty yourself before you leave in the morning. It will be eight o'clock to catch the eight-thirty tube. Your appointment is at ten in Regent's Street."

Veronica had not missed Mrs Jenkins exact wording. The first instance obviously referred to peeing. "And what of the second instance?"

"You must have a thorough enema before you get dressed."

"What's that?"

Mrs Jenkins looked mortified and glanced at Polly, who nodded. "Do we have the equipment?"

"Equipment?" said Veronica looking from one to the other.

"It is in her mother's bedroom. I was reminded. I would also suggest that you do it in the attached bathroom, for there will be no interruption and it is more easily cleaned."

Veronica's mind was assailed with recollections of the tortures she had suffered in the attempts to straighten her back. "What are you going to do to me?"

Polly smiled. "Pump water up your bum to clear you out so you don't need to go at some inconvenient moment. All the ladies in town do it."

———— ◉ ————

IT WAS DECIDED, NOT by Veronica, that it would be best to have a test run after lunch so that they could be practised for the morning.

And good as their word, after she had eaten and comfortably digested the cold meats with cheese and delicious bread prepared for lunch, Veronica was taken back to her parents' room.

"Ring the bell when you're done," said Mrs Jenkins. "And I will let you out."

With that she closed the door and the key clicked in the lock. Veronica felt trapped.

"Let me undress you," said Polly.

"I don't want to do this."

"It'll be fine."

"I'm scared." She glanced around the room. "And I don't like it in here."

"I'll be gentle."

Veronica was not reassured. She was reminded of another promise the girl had made which had not turned out to be the truth—even if it was understandable.

Polly unbuttoned the dress and helped Veronica out of it. This was followed by the chemise, drawers, shoes and stockings. Naked and feeling vulnerable in the strange room, Veronica wrapped her arms around herself and perched on the edge of the bed while Polly fetched a leather case from the dressing room.

"Let's go in the other room."

So Veronica followed her maid into the tiled bathroom with its roll-top, enamelled tub. Above it intricate plumbing allowed water to be heated in a small stove as it was fed down into the bath.

"I think it'll be easier to clean up if you're in the bath when we do this."

Veronica gave Polly a pleading look in an effort to communicate how much she did *not* want to do this. But Polly just held out her hand for Veronica to grab as she climbed over the high side into the tub.

"Do you want me to sit down?"

Polly considered. "No, I think it would be best if you were on your knees facing away from the taps and plughole."

Veronica obliged and rested her arms on the edge. Polly opened the leather case.

"Let me see," said Veronica. "I want to know what you're going to be shoving into me this time."

Polly brought out a device with a green rubber bladder at one end, a tube covered with a tight woven material, in matching green, which terminated in a silvery attachment that had a valve at one end and a bulbous tip at the other.

Polly held up the attachment. "This end goes in your bum. I fill the bulb with water and attach it to the tube. We let the air bubble up to the top, open the valve and I squeeze to make the water go in."

"Give me the tube," said Veronica. It was quite light and the metal was very smooth. "How do you know so much about it?"

Polly was filling the bulb, and Veronica guessed it would probably take a pint in total.

"Some doctors like women to have them before they give birth, I've seen it used."

"Why?"

"Because pushing a baby out is like having a poo. And when a baby comes out of one hole and you know what comes out of the other."

Veronica sighed. Being a woman really wasn't a lot of fun. Except for the lust, that was fun. The only thing she did that gave her any real pleasure.

"I've brought some vaseline so it can go in more easily."

Polly brought the full bulb over and put it down in the tub behind Veronica. The window was closed and the sun shone through it. There was a fly trying to get out and its intermittent buzzing was irritating. Eventually, thought Veronica, it will dehydrate and die. And it will have no idea why.

Something cold touched her bum hole and she jumped.

"Sorry," said Polly. "I'm going to work it around a bit and then I'll push some inside."

"I am really looking forward to it," said Veronica beneath her breath, but her maid must have heard.

"Are you?" She sounded surprised.

"No, I'm not, now if you would just get on with it?"

Veronica braced herself. Polly's finger came down on her anus again and went round and around. Veronica's eyes widened in surprise. This was not unpleasant at all. In fact it was quite stimulating. She once again despaired of the perverse nature of female biology and then relaxed into the pleasant sensation.

Polly removed her finger.

"Oh," said Veronica except it was the sound of disappointment.

"What now?"

"You stopped."

"I'd finished."

"You..." Veronica trailed off.

"What?"

"You could do it some more?" She let her words form a question rather than a demand, because she was still surprised at the effect.

"You enjoyed it," Polly's statement was almost one of disgust. "After all your complaining."

"I didn't know."

"You sound like a child."

"Well, I didn't."

"All right, just for a bit, but we have to do the enema."

"I know," said Veronica. She placed her forearms and hand on the edge of the bath then turned her head to the side and rested her head on them. "Just for a little while."

Polly's finger returned to Veronica's anus and stroked it gently. She ran it around the outside and then moved her fingers up the crack and then back, down the crack towards Veronica's quim and then back. Veronica gave a little moan every time Polly's finger was doing something particularly pleasant, to encourage her to do it more.

"Press harder. I think I could come," she said finally. Polly obliged and Veronica's muscles were pressed inward as the girl massaged her bum hole more vigorously. "Put your finger in me."

"In your bum?" Polly's voice cracked slightly as she spoke and Veronica smiled to herself. If she was not much mistaken, Miss Polly was getting stimulated herself. Perhaps she might like having her anus massaged too.

"You were going to anyway..."

Polly didn't argue. Her fingers went round and round Veronica's rear opening and then pushed gently in. It went in easily at first and then stopped. Veronica groaned with pleasure. "Don't stop."

The tension in her behind increased as Polly pushed harder. She pulled back and then pushed again. Veronica could feel her wriggling her finger around trying to find the entrance point. Then she removed her hand completely.

"Please don't stop."

"More vaseline," said Polly in clipped tones. And moments later her fingers were back and spreading more of the jelly in and around Veronica's anus.

Veronica squeezed her thighs and brought pressure to bear on her nubbin. The electricity of lust shot through her. Polly pushed hard. Her finger broke through the barrier, and Veronica let out a moan that came from deep inside.

"Move it," she ordered. "In and out like you're fucking me."

The push and pull on her anal nerves was made Veronica feel as if she would explode. She squeezed her nubbin and pushed back against Polly's finger. "Put more in me!"

There was a moment's fumbling and the stretching of her anus as two fingers went in.

"Oh god," panted Veronica. She pushed back hard in rhythm with Polly's thrusts. She leaned up with one hand on the tub and with the other she pulled at her tits. She shrieked and came. Her pulsing contractions both in her cunt and in her anus, tightening rhythmically on Polly's fingers.

Veronica let her head drop back on to her arm and felt Polly pulling out her fingers. "No, wait, just leave them for a moment."

Veronica's panting slowed and her awareness returned.

"Can I take them out now?"

Veronica grunted which Polly took for a yes and withdrew her fingers. Veronica felt empty.

"I have got your poo on my fingers," said Polly.

"Sorry."

"This is why we do an enema," she said getting up and going to the sink. Water ran.

"So you can put your fingers up my bum and not get them dirty?" said Veronica.

"Very funny."

"I might want you to do that again."

"In that case we shall be making an enema a regular part of your regime," said Polly, returning. "And no shoving of fingers up your behind until afterwards."

"Except for the vaseline."

"Mmm," said Polly in a disapproving way. "Now you just stay still and let me do this."

Moments later the cold metal nozzle was pressed against her anus. "Ready?"

"Yes."

Polly pushed and it slipped in easily. It gave Veronica another frisson of pleasure. She shivered as it went deeper. It was longer than Polly's fingers and bigger, the sensation of having something big and solid in that hole was pleasant indeed. The thought of something like that going in and out of her bum was most stimulating.

The cold water was not.

She did not realise what it was at first but the feeling of heaviness and fullness increased and the sensation of needing to defecate became stronger.

"Hold it in," said Polly as if she knew what was happening. "I've nearly got the whole lot in you."

Something ached inside. Veronica grimaced. "It hurts."

"Just keep it in."

Veronica heard her move away and there was running taps again. Shortly after she was back. The pressure seemed to be diminishing and the desire to eject the entire contents of her body was less intense.

And then it came back.

"What are you doing?"

"Second load."

"That's a quart!"

"You can take it, you're a big girl."

Veronica groaned, this time in pain. "Is this more revenge?"

"Oh no, this is what you need. There, it's all in now."

She did something and the tube came away with the attachment still stuck up her bum. Veronica wondered how she could possibly have imagined that it was pleasurable. She felt like she had diarrhoea. Polly turned on one of the taps in the bath and the water tumbled noisily onto the ceramic surface.

"I'm going to take the end out of you," she said. "Keep holding it in."

The attachment slid out of her bum and Veronica clamped down on the water that tried to gush out.

"Good girl," said Polly.

"How long do I have to hold it? It's like muscle cramps."

The water from the taps was lapping round her toes and she was getting tired in this position.

Polly came round to her end of the bath. She smiled. "Take my hands and lean back until you're straight."

"Straight?" growled Veronica.

Polly did not take offence or look guilty. "You know what I mean."

Veronica followed her instructions until she kneeling upright. Polly bent over, kissed her on the lips and then on the nose.

"Let it go."

xxxii

The following morning, early, Mrs Jenkins let them back into the master bedroom where Veronica was given another enema. This time it was only a single bulb and the result was not as disgusting as it had been the day before. There was also no time for play, though the application of vaseline had possibly taken a little longer than it needed to.

Veronica was dressed for travel—a tricky proposition since she had not the clothes for it. In the end they decided on a walking dress she wore on Sundays. It was a very dowdy brown colour with a high neck.

The day was already hot and humid by the time Veronica, Polly and Mrs Jenkins climbed into the carriage. Veronica thought Mrs Jenkins in particular had not taken the heat of the day into account and she was even wearing a coat. Polly was also in her Sunday Best since that was her only decent alternative to her uniform.

For Veronica the whole thing evoked such mixed emotions she did not know where to put herself. She was excited about getting out of the house, and even more so since she was heading up to London. She had read Dickens and the magazines but she had never expected to have the chance to be there.

And she was scared. There were so many people in London. For her it was a crowd when four people were together in a room. The photographs in the weeklies showed streets with thousands of people walking at the sides of the roads, not to mention hundreds of carriages.

Then there was the fact she was going to be measured for a wedding dress, and she really did not know what to think about that. The prospect of being suddenly in charge of the house she had grown up in.

Ultimately there was also her hump. People would stare at her. London would stare at her. And they would despise her as everyone did.

The carriage was not open and through the small windows she saw they had come to the town and it was only moments later they passed one of the tube pumping stations. The horses slowed and came to a halt at the side of the station.

Mrs Jenkins descended first, then Polly who helped Veronica down.

Exposed to the world Veronica wanted to climb back inside and hide, but there was no time for that. Mrs Jenkins led the way to the ticket office and purchased three first-class returns. She then made enquiries of the staff to find out which end of the platform they should stand.

Veronica stared through the windows at the curved surface of the riveted iron tube that ran along the platform. At intervals along its length there were doors, closed now. When the train arrived the inner doors would line up with the outer ones and both would open simultaneously.

She glanced at the clock: it was due in a few minutes.

Once more the housekeeper led the way out to the platform and headed north along its length. The platform was not empty. Men in suits of different qualities stood alone or in small groups. Some reading newspapers, one or two talking in quiet tones. Towards the southern end were men in cheap suits and some in overalls. A woman waited quietly while two children played peekaboo around her skirts.

Veronica stared at them for a short while. She could not imagine herself having children. Such a thing was as far from her mind as marriage had been a couple of weeks ago. Though she was now much better educated on the process of making children, she still could not imagine being able to bring them up.

The tube in front of them vibrated and the sound of roaring filled the air. The tube trains were pushed along by the pneumatics of air under pressure. The pumping station at the southern part of the station pushed the air through. There were flexible valves at intervals that only allowed the air to flow in one direction so the trains could keep moving.

At stations there were subsidiary tubes that led up to the station platform while the main line continued through the middle. And there were lines in both directions of course. Properly they were called the Brunel Pneumatic Railway System, but everyone just called them the Tube, because that's what they were.

The ironwork thundered as the steam engine that led the train of carriages passed by coming to a halt. An electrical generator was required to power the lights and, more importantly, the Faraday grid that stretched the length of the entire train.

There were windows in both the tube and the carriages, which also lined up. The whole machine came to a halt and after a few moments of mechanical thumping and bumping the doors slid back. One person got off the carriage that they had selected. He looked like another of the same breed from which Mr Slack, the elder and younger, had been made. He glanced at them but since clearly none of them was of any rank he simply walked past.

Veronica felt that his eyes had lingered on her a little longer than the others, but, she reminded herself, she must get used to it. Everyone in London would stare at her gross deformity.

There was a passage, just wide enough for two people to pass one another, that ran along the side of compartments in the first class section. Their tickets were for a ladies compartment closest to the engine.

Although there was sunlight streaming through the windows on the far side, Veronica was impressed by the illumination supplied by the electric lights. To think they would have this at the house soon. Contrary to what she had been told there was a sign to a Ladies Toilet which, she assumed, would also include a water closet.

The ladies carriage had a bench for seating on each side which were divided into four wide seats by generously padded armrests. Everything was upholstered in leather which had been stained the green of the London, Brighton and South Coast Railway who operated this line.

There was no one else in the carriage and Mrs Jenkins allowed Veronica and Polly to sit on opposite sides nearest the windows.

Shortly afterwards one of the station officers blew a whistle and the doors slammed shut with a crash that rocked the carriage. A klaxon sounded briefly through the train. Veronica saw Mrs Jenkins grab the armrests in a grip that made her knuckles go white. For a moment she had no idea why but then it happened.

For the briefest moment she felt as if she was falling. Polly cried out and looked scared but Veronica was elated. It was the Faraday device engaging throughout the train. Everything became lighter.

Seth was right! The moment it happened she felt the strain go from her back, she lifted slightly on the springs in the seat because she no longer weighed as much.

She wanted to experiment with this new wonder and stood up; she flew upwards and barely had time to raise her hands before striking the ceiling. She had not noticed before but even the ceiling was padded. Probably only in first class.

She fell back to the ground to see Polly's look of horror and amazement. Veronica's face was in a wide smile and then she was crying.

"What's wrong?" said Polly. She may have been concerned but she still gripped the padded arms just like Mrs Jenkins.

"Nothing," said Veronica. "Nothing at all. It's wonderful."

xxxiii

The train stopped at a dozen more stations where the Faraday had been switched on and off, giving Veronica the opportunity to appreciate it more than once. No women came into their carriage and only the conductor disturbed them to check their tickets. After an hour and a half they arrived at London Bridge station where the LB & SC Railway train terminated.

Veronica's head swam as she stepped out onto the platform into a tide of hundreds of people most of whom had alighted from the train and were heading in the same direction, but others were going back the other way. There seemed to be no pattern and no rhyme or reason. She felt as if she would drown in the confusion.

It was worse because she was bent over and could not see further than a few people. And they touched her, or rather they brushed past.

"Polly?" she said, her voice lost in the noise of engines and steam, and of people talking and shouting. How could anyone communicate in this? "Polly!"

A small hand slipped into hers and Veronica gripped it convulsively.

"I'm here."

"This way," came the commanding tone of Mrs Jenkins as she swept off along the platform. Veronica latched her eyes onto her rear and followed it as closely as she could, fearful that someone might come between them and they would lose her.

"It's all right," said Polly in her ear. "I can see her well enough."

They reached the ticket barrier where the crowds turned into something like an orderly queue. Mrs Jenkins handed their tickets to the collector and they went through into the station proper. The press became less as people stopped brushing past and gave them some space.

Mrs Jenkins strode ahead and managed to accost a porter. She enquired how they could get to Regent's Street. He was not impolite but he was curt, taking in the group of three women, and his eyes lingering for a moment on Veronica as she closed the distance to Mrs Jenkins.

"There's no underground direct from here, and you'd have to go to Oxford Circus or Piccadilly Circus depending on which end you want. Both of them are on the Bakerloo line so you'd have to get the Northern down to Elephant and Castle first."

It meant nothing to Veronica and she was not sure that Mrs Jenkins understood either.

"Is there an easier way?"

"You can take a cab from outside the station," he said, pointing towards a great wall ahead of them punctured by arches and windows.

Mrs Jenkins tipped him and, after glancing back to ensure the girls were still with her, she headed out.

There was a queue for the cab and within moments they were sandwiched between a pair of suited gentlemen in conversation, and there was the woman with the two children who had been at the station where Veronica had got on.

She was still having trouble with the constant battering her ears were getting from thundering trains, horses, steam carriages and shouting; while her nose was assailed by horse dung, coal smoke and diesel fumes. The heat of the day was making it worse. The place was stifling.

"I am rapidly forming the opinion that I do not like London," she said to Polly, though it seemed Mrs Jenkins had heard too.

"I'm sure it will be your only visit," said Mrs Jenkins.

The queue moved rapidly and they were soon at the head of it. The next cab in the queue came forward. A compact machine with what Veronica took for a diesel engine, since it wasn't steam and it belched black smoke.

If any of them had expected the driver to open the door for them they were disappointed, but since none of the people earlier in the queue had received that courtesy it was not a surprise.

Mrs Jenkins fought with the handle and got the door open. All three climbed in and Mrs Jenkins gave the address. The cab did possess a Faraday device, which engaged as they pulled away but it was low efficiency and, though she became a little lighter, Veronica did not get much respite from the ache in her back.

Unlike the carriage they had taken to the station this vehicle had large windows and Veronica was able to observe the insanity that was London. For a start the roads were packed with traffic of all sorts, from men on horseback to unnaturally huge lorries piled high with goods—they must be using Faraday devices to allow them to carry such huge loads. There were omnibuses, some with open tops, private carriages, and machines she could only describe as road trains: steam-drawn chains of carriages carrying passengers and other goods.

Mingling with these and seemingly crossing roads at random were the pedestrians. That none of them were run-down by the powered vehicles was astonishing. It was like a maelstrom in the heart of chaos.

After leaving London Bridge station they passed along a road lined with warehousing on one side and business premises on the other with their company names emblazoned across the frontages. At a busy junction they turned right and were soon crossing the long arch of Waterloo Bridge.

The waters of the Thames were busy with traffic and now that she could see further, the sky too was busy with all manner of flying vehicles. In the distance, just as the river made a long bend there was the Tower of St Stephen housing the bell Big Ben. The building from which it emerged had once housed the British Parliament but that had moved to Manchester twenty years before, despite the protests of the old Queen.

But soon enough they were across the bridge and now into a less industrial area—although the quantity of traffic did not change its quality did with fewer lorries and more smaller vehicles.

After only a short time she lost her bearings, though the driver clearly knew the route. She caught sight of several theatres showing an assortment of plays including one by the notorious Bernard Shaw, and then they were on a long straight road. It was filled with omnibuses, cabs and pedestrians. The buildings on each side were just shops, dozens of shops of every variety. Some she even recognised as advertising in the magazines she read.

Oxford Street.

She wished they could take some time and wander along, taking it all in. But that was not going to happen, not if Mrs Jenkins had anything to do with it.

At a huge crossroads they turned left again—she saw the road sign that proclaimed them to be in Regent's Street—and almost immediately left again into a back road and then right to parallel the main road but down an arcade with smaller, even more expensive shops.

Finally the cab came to a halt and the Faraday device cut out. Polly got out and helped Veronica while Mrs Jenkins settled the fare. The foot traffic was not so dense here and it seemed pedestrians had the right of way. The cab was the only wheeled vehicle in sight and it quickly disappeared from view.

Mrs Jenkins consulted her directions and then looked at the shops.

"This way."

xxxiv

The House of Jeanne Paquin, *couturier* to gentry across Europe, was a place of quiet and calm after the chaos of the London streets. The smell was of perfume—undefinable yet refined—while the staff, all young ladies, wore uniforms, but they were long and flowing as if they were the latest fashion.

But as refined as they might be, as she entered Veronica saw them hesitate as they saw her. She could divine the nature of a person by the way they looked at her. Pity was the most common, repugnance the next, but the truth was that neither such people wanted to have anything to do with her. She had experienced little else in her lifetime.

Of course they did not give Polly a second glance. It seemed a shop girl considered herself to be above a Lady's maid. Well, at present she looked like a maid dressed in her Sunday Best to come up to town.

Veronica realised that Polly probably felt even more uncomfortable than she did. Even without her training in etiquette she was sure that holding hands with a maid would be frowned on but she didn't care. Polly was right there next to her and Veronica took her hand and gave it a little squeeze. She received one in return.

An older woman, still in the uniform of the shop, came forward.

"Clifford-Hughes party?" she said in smooth tones that had a hint of a French accent about it.

Mrs Jenkins was also intimidated, for all she did was nod.

"This way please, madame, mademoiselle."

She turned and led the way into the back of the shop and up a very tight flight of stairs. The stairs continued up but they went along a short passage and into a room where the walls were lined with partially made dresses.

"Mademoiselle Madeleine Vionnet will take care of your requirements."

So much for getting Jeanne Paquin, thought Veronica. Clearly she did not rate that high. From behind a desk a tall blonde woman stood. Her hair was cut short and clung to her head in rolls. Such a modern style it looked outrageous.

But the woman's dress clung and moved in a way Veronica had never seen. Not that she had not had much interest in women's clothing, until now.

The woman, in her thirties, held out her hand to Veronica. "Good morning, Miss Clifford-Jones. It is a pleasure to meet you."

She was too close for Veronica to look up into her face. It was frustrating.

Releasing her hand, the woman introduced herself to both Mrs Jenkins and Polly—Miss Noakes. Veronica realised until now she had not even known Polly's surname. It had never even occurred to her to ask.

"This will take some time, Mrs Jenkins, if you are happy to leave your charge in my care perhaps you would like to spend some time in the shops?"

Veronica was not sure how the housekeeper would take it but it seemed she was happy with the suggestion and, after telling Veronica to do exactly as she was told, she left.

"Let us sit," said Madeleine. In that position, a short distance apart and at a better level Veronica was able to see the woman properly. She was not wearing any shoes.

"You see," said Miss Vionnet. "You have been given to me because no one else in the House is willing to have their clothes on the body of someone they do not consider fit to wear them."

"I understand," said Veronica. Polly's hand came down on hers and held it. The motion was not lost on Miss Vionnet. "If you do not wish to make my dress I imagine we can make do."

Madeleine laughed in a short harsh back. "You British and your 'make do'. No, Miss Clifford-Hughes, Veronica. I shall make a dress for you that will make them all jealous."

"Please don't put yourself out, nobody will see it. The wedding is going to be very small." She hesitated for a moment. "*Very* small."

"Are you with child?"

"No, of course not, that's a very impertinent question."

"And important. Should I make a dress that fits you now but not at the altar?"

Veronica frowned. "I am not pregnant."

"*Bien sur*, and what about bridesmaids?"

"No."

"What about your lover?" She looked pointedly at Polly.

Veronica opened her mouth to deny it, but no words came out.

"I can speak for myself," said Polly, as if she were defending Veronica's honour.

Madeleine smiled. "And are you happy she is to be married?"

"It's not up to me."

Miss Vionnet shrugged. "Whatever you say. I will not make a bridal gown without a bridesmaid's dress to go with it."

Mrs Jenkins' most likely objection sprang to Veronica's lips. "What about the cost?"

Again the shrug. "Your future mother-in-law is paying, though she has not ordered a dress for the event so I assume she is not attending."

Veronica shook her head.

"There will, of course, be hair to be made up and cosmetics. And you will be barefoot."

"Barefoot?" said Veronica, thinking of the cold stones of the church.

"You say yourself no one is going to see, what difference does it make?"

Veronica had no answer but she still had one objection. "I don't want to spoil your creation, Miss Vionnet. You have seen this." She nodded slightly to the right to indicate her hump.

"It is nothing but a challenge. Come, we will begin." She stood up. "Disrobe completely. I must see everything."

If she expected Veronica to protest she was disappointed. With Polly's assistance, she was soon standing naked on a small stool in the middle of the room with Polly holding her hand to keep her balance.

"Very good," said Miss Vionnet as she moved around taking measurements. "You will require new undergarments, you cannot wear these disgusting things beneath my creation. Now I will touch your, what is it? Hump?"

Veronica braced herself. So many times she had been prodded and twisted without any regard to the pain inflicted. But Madeleine simply ran her hands across her body.

"Is this incurable?" the older woman asked.

"There were attempts when I was younger. They hurt me."

"I see," she went back to her desk and picked up a pad. She wandered around making quick sketches. Veronica caught a glimpse of one, it didn't look anything like her.

"Very well," said Madeleine. "You may get dressed. And your maid can take your place."

"Me?" said Polly.

"If you are to have a bridesmaid dress designed by Vionnet then yes, you will stand on that pedestal with no clothes and I will measure you."

Polly looked at Veronica in horror. "If there is no bridesmaid, Vionnet will not make my dress."

"But…"

"And," said Vionnet. "If you are in need of money you can sell the dress and live for a year."

"Don't worry about getting me dressed," said Veronica. "Do it quickly."

Polly stripped and stood while Madeleine measured and sketched. It took less time than it had for Veronica but Polly was clearly suffering from intense embarrassment. So Veronica held her hand.

Madeleine smiled at them.

Finally it was done. The *couturier* put her pad back and watched the two of them get dressed. As the underwear went on, she tutted. "You English have such an archaic sense of style."

"We don't appreciate being insulted by the French," said Veronica.

"But our countries have an *Entente Cordiale*," said Miss Vionnet. "It means I can insult you all I wish without there being a war."

Veronica laughed. "You are very arrogant, Miss Vionnet."

"I am a *couturier*, Miss Clifford-Hughes. I make fashion."

"But you're working for Jeanne Paquin."

"Not for much longer, if you are able to keep a secret," she said.

"I have no one I can tell," said Veronica.

"Next year I shall be opening my temple of fashion in Paris. Then we shall see who leads the world."

"And will the dress you made for a deformed gargoyle feature in your history?"

Miss Vionnet smiled. "All women are beautiful, Miss Clifford-Jones. It is my task to make the world realise it."

XXXV

A tremendous crash woke Veronica from her deep sleep. The air was split with a thunder that did not fade but grew constantly louder. The bed was shuddering with vibrations transmitted through the walls and floors. The curtains were drawn but sunlight streamed through the gaps.

She reached out and her hand landed on soft flesh. It made her jump. She pushed herself up on her elbow and realised that she was sharing her bed with Polly. She hadn't been there when Veronica had gone to sleep.

When did she arrive? What was the time? *And what in God's name was that noise?*

Something porcelain crashed to the floor across the room and shattered. The windows were thudding as the sound beat against them from outside. A huge shadow moved across the sun casting its slow-moving shade along the curtains.

It was almost like London all over again. She had the crazy idea that the city had somehow followed back to the house.

Polly moved and her arms snaked out and around Veronica's body. The girl pulled and Veronica toppled over on top of her. Polly moved her legs so that Veronica's thigh was trapped between hers. Veronica squirmed but Polly crossed her ankles so Veronica was unable to move her leg. Lying on top of Polly, Veronica could not lift her head to see. The thundering continued outside as if the trumpets of Joshua's army were trying to bring down the house.

"Polly, for Heaven's sake, can't you hear the noise?" She almost had to shout to make her voice carry over the cacophony.

Polly's only response was to kiss and then nibble Veronica's neck—which was delicious and distracting but not what she wanted.

"The noise!" she shouted in Polly's ear which was just below her mouth. At another time she might have nibbled her lobe.

"Workmen," said Polly back into Veronica's ear. "Ignore them."

She then moved down in the bed until she was able to grab Veronica's breast and feed it into her mouth. She sucked and then ground her teeth on her mistress's nipple.

Veronica's body went rigid with the pleasure of it. *God damn her.* One of Polly's hands found its way between Veronica's thighs and rubbed her. *Not fair.* Veronica tried to focus but the noise seemed to fade as her body's demands became more important. She pushed against the mattress and brought sat back pulling her quim out of Polly's hands but landing in a kneeling position pressing her delta against her maid's knee. She obligingly raised it while Veronica moved her hips back and forth rubbing her nubbin.

With her hands now free Polly reached up and scratched her nails across the peaks of Veronica's breasts. Whether it was because she had missed out on any lustful activities the day before, Veronica felt herself rising towards the peak very quickly.

She did not slow down.

Her hands were on Polly's hips as she ground into the maid's leg. She moved slightly and brought her own knee up into Polly's groin, giving her something to press against. In response she felt Polly rotating her lower body against the new stimulus. Polly grabbed Veronica's tit and jammed her nails into it. Veronica whimpered with the pain that shot through her redoubling her pleasure.

Her maid's chest was rising and falling in quick breaths as she approached her peak. The look in her eyes was a glazed determination. She twisted and pulled Veronica's nipple as if she was going to rip it off.

"Ow," said Veronica, "don't stop."

As Polly tore at the other nipple, making Veronica close her eyes at the delightful agony, she moved forward along Polly's leg, lifting the other one until it was upright past her ear. Polly gave a slight frown as if she did not quite understand what Veronica was doing. As Veronica moved further up her pinned leg, the free one was pointed skyward. Until their quims came in contact.

Polly smiled.

The thundering of the engines outside continued to drown out any lesser noise.

In unison, they rubbed against one another. They made each other slick as they rotated their groins into each other. Veronica dug the fingers of her right hand into the maid's stomach and with her left grabbed Polly's bum. She slipped her fingers into the crack which was slick with their juices.

She touched her maid's anus. The girl's eyes went wide but she did not stop pressing herself against Veronica. The flush of lust had spread across her chest and neck. In time with their movements against one another Veronica pressed her finger into the girl's bum. She pushed back and her movements became more spasmodic. She tried to maintain the rhythm as she headed towards her peak.

Veronica smiled when Polly closed her eyes, her entire being devoted to the sensations pouring from between her legs and out through her entire body. She was grunting with every breath. Her rear was moving against Veronica's finger and each thrust pushed it a little deeper. The grip of her anus so tight Veronica thought she might cut off the blood circulation.

Polly started to pant and her hands clamped around Veronica's wrist in an iron grip. Veronica kept thrusting with her hips as an unfamiliar whine broke from Polly's lips. Her head was thrown back, the muscles in her anus began to spasm, Veronica shoved her finger in and out of her rear as best she could against the tight muscles.

The whine turned into a choking scream. Polly's leg muscles vibrated and she went rigid. She was not even breathing. After a few seconds Veronica became concerned, then Polly took a breath and went limp. The grip on Veronica's wrist and her finger relaxed.

Gently Veronica slid her finger from Polly's behind, she gave it a quick check. It looked clean. Then she moved Polly's leg from her shoulder and let it down gently to the bed. Polly was either unconscious, exhausted or asleep. Veronica moved back and separated their groins. A few of her dark hairs were stuck to Polly's quim. Both of them were very wet and there was a patch of damp on the sheet. Not the first, but considerably more than usual.

Veronica looked towards the window. The noise was clearly machinery, and she guessed a flying machine, but what was going on?

Her knees were stiff but she managed to climb off Polly and padded naked across to the windows. She moved the curtain aside a little and peeked out.

In the field beyond the garden was indeed a flying machine with "The Brunel Company" painted on its side. With a rotor at each corner she knew it was one of the vehicles that could take off and land vertically. The rotors twisted to the horizontal when it was in flight to provide forward motion.

There were Sky Liners of enormous size of a similar design but this was a cargo vessel—not that it was small. A huge hatch had been opened in its side and a machine as big as her room was being unloaded on to a big steam truck. Both the machine and the truck were also painted with the Brunel name.

Arms wrapped round her waist and she felt a pair of breasts pressing into her back. Polly's cheek came to rest on her shoulder.

"Thank you."

A smile twitched on Veronica's face. "You seemed to enjoy it."

"Are you fishing for compliments, Mistress Nika?"

"Perhaps."

"I think you can tell I enjoyed it."

"Even when I put my finger in that place?"

Polly hesitated. "I suppose."

They went quiet and peeked through the gap, watching the workmen—there were at least twenty they could see—helping to manhandle the machine into place.

"Did you know this was going to happen today?" said Veronica.

"Of course."

"Well, nobody mentioned it to me," she said. "I was confused and when you ignored it I thought I must be going mad and just imagining it."

"Sorry, Nika," said Polly. "What is that anyway?"

"Oh, so you don't actually know what it is?"

"Do you?"

"It's either the electrical generator or the furnace," she said confidently. "Or perhaps both."

There was a thud from inside the house.

"Now what?"

"Your husband-to-be is rearranging the interior as well."

Veronica frowned. "Oh well, I suppose it's a small price to pay to get electricity in the house, and it will be over eventually."

"Do you want a bath before you face the world?"

"What day is it?"

"Wednesday."

"I suppose I shall be having lessons with Mr Plumley. What are my feet like?"

"After traipsing all over London yesterday? Quite bad I should think."

Veronica said nothing.

"You cannot seriously expect me to get down there and smell your feet."

"I had yours by my ear this morning."

"And how bad was it?"

"I was too busy giving you the most perfect attainment of pleasure you have ever experienced to notice."

"Are you blackmailing me?" said Polly.

"I believe that is the term."

Rather than simply letting go then getting on her hands and knees, Polly loosened her grip and slid down Veronica's body, stroking and kissing as she went.

She sniffed her mistress's feet.

"Well?"

"Not sure, they're certainly a bit stale but I'm no expert in Mr Plumley's preferencies." She got back to her feet and went to the chair where she had left her clothes.

"Have you put my stocking from yesterday in the laundry yet?"

"They're over there with the rest of your clothes from yesterday."

"I'll wear the same stockings and shoes, but get the stockings a bit wet before you put them on me. That should do the trick."

"Yes," said Polly. "You're very good at coming up with ideas to make your feet smell."

xxxvi

As it turned out Mr Plumley had been very pleased with the ripe state of her feet but there had been some trouble over the arrangements.

Both the building and the gardens were full of workmen. It was as if they were living in the middle of a building site. Scaffolding was being erected outside. Outhouses being refurbished and their purposes reassigned. Inside, men were taking sledgehammers to walls on both floors.

At first Mr Plumley did not even want to entertain the idea of licking her feet, even though he clearly wanted to. It was almost tragic to see the way he was torn between desire and fear of discovery.

The door being locked was not an issue, it was even more justifiable since they did not want workmen coming in and disturbing Veronica at her lessons. But he was concerned about the curtains. Polly had pulled them closed but there were gaps and Mr Plumley had it in his head that the workmen would be bound to peer inside in order to discover what was being hidden from them.

If there was something that appeared to be a secret then people would want to know what was there, even if it was nothing.

Veronica was not entirely sure why she was insisting; after all, she got no especial pleasure from his attentions. She did however think it was important, partly because she still felt she owed him for what he had done—even though it may have become superfluous—and because she did rather enjoy having a man worshipping at her feet. It made a change from the disgust.

In the end he was persuaded by having her seated at the table as if she was working, while he got underneath it, as he had that first day. Then if anyone was to look through the window they would see Veronica and they would be unable to see him.

In fact the idea of that gave an extra *frisson* to the whole affair: that she could be seen and no one would know she was having her feet licked.

And so it was. Mr Plumley was very happy with the state of her feet and, afterwards, enquired whether she would be going up to London again. She did not want to disappoint him but felt honesty was the best policy and admitted that she thought it unlikely.

"B-b-but why do you s-say that, M-mistress Nika?" He climbed to his feet on the other side of the table and brushed down his trousers. Veronica peered at his groin, as far as she could see he was not excited by his activities with her feet.

"Because I have had my dress fitting, there's no reason to go again."

"And w-what is to s-stop you?"

She stared at him as he sat down. Once again he was her tutor only. Behind her, Polly unlocked the door and went to pull the curtains back. The shouts of workmen echoed round the building.

"What is to stop me, sir? All the things that prevented me before."

"I can s-see, M-miss Clifford-Hughes, you have not thought through this m-marriage b-business at all. M-may I s-say once again: if you ch-choose to go up to London, w-what is to s-stop you?"

Veronica frowned and stared at the desk in front of her. Her feet were still damp from the licking and bare against the wood of the parquet flooring.

"Oh dear, I b-believed you w-were cleverer than this," he said with a shake of his head. "Or p-perhaps you are like an animal that has been k-kept in a c-cage its entire life, and when the door is opened it does not leave."

The light dawned slowly. "I require the permission of my husband."

"And w-what is his nature?"

She had met him twice, and really only spoken to him once at any length. And his general attitude? "He cares whether things suit him, but if they have no relation to him I do not think he gives them any mind whatsoever."

What Mr Plumley had said was true, she realised, but considerably worse than he imagined. Until the last month or so she had not realised there was a cage; when she realised she was imprisoned she had not believed there was a door. So, indeed no, when the door had been opened it was not a fear of leaving that kept her inside, she had not realised the door was even there.

Though the cage was broken and dismantled around her, she still felt its walls.

"In the tropics," said Mr Plumley, "there are f-fishermen that net their c-catch with sh-shadows."

"Is that so?" she said with no small amount of harshness in her tone.

Mr Plumley continued as if she had not commented. "They thread pieces of w-wood on to a rope and float it on the water. The f-fish see the shadow and b-b-believe it is real. They think they c-cannot escape. The rope is drawn into the sh-shallows where the f-fish are caught."

"The bars of my cage were real, Mr Plumley."

"W-were they? Or did you s-simply b-b-believe they were?"

Veronica found herself getting angry. "What is it we are studying now, Mr Plumley?"

"Ph-ph-philosophy. The American School of P-pragmatists."

"I do not care for it."

"It is a difficult s-subject," he said. "It requires self-examination, and a consideration of consequences." He took up his briefcase and fished a pamphlet from it. He pushed it across the table to her. "An introduction. Read it b-by tomorrow, I w-will test you."

"Some parts of the cage remain," said Veronica.

Mr Plumley smiled.

xxxvii

The chaos caused by the changes demanded by her future husband meant that morning assignations with Seth were impossible. The workmen were up earlier than she was, using every moment of daylight for their work.

The house was filled from end to end with noise and bustle and dirt. The maids were kept working full time on keeping a semblance of tidiness about the place. But when walls were being knocked down, holes made, doorways bricked up, windows removed, doors replaced—it became almost impossible to even think.

The only benefit Veronica was able to gain from the upset was to arrange for Polly to stay with her day and night.

"Out of the question," said Mrs Jenkins when Veronica declared her desire in the housekeeper's office. It crossed Veronica's mind that Mrs Jenkins and Mr Laughton's lustful desires must also be under pressure. There would be no opportunity for them to fuck either.

"I am afraid."

That declaration caught the older woman without a retort so Veronica pressed on.

"The house is full of strange men, and while they may be required to leave during the night their camp is only in the field. What is to stop one of them returning in the night?"

Mrs Jenkins did not respond again, though Veronica was certain that it was not a realisation of threat that stopped her. Could it be that Mrs Jenkins would *like* to meet one of those rough men in the night? In fact, now she came to think about it, Veronica also thought that might be interesting, though she really had her compass set on Seth. She felt she would rather know a man when she allowed him into her body.

"You make a good point," said Mrs Jenkins and for a moment Veronica was confused about what she was responding to. Obviously not her thought about only fucking men she knew—not that she had done it with even one yet—oh, yes, she had mentioned the threat.

"Thank you."

"You have bolts on your door now." That comment was almost an accusation and there was the silent follow-up about not having any dangerous plants in her room even though that was the original reason.

"It does not prevent me from being scared," said Veronica. "My parents wanted me to have a sheltered upbringing and I am very unused to this." She gestured all round and, conveniently, the shouting broke out as she did so. Then something crashed to the ground outside. Both of them jumped.

"Very well, she can stay in your room."

Veronica frowned. It had not been a request but never mind, the point had been ceded.

"She will require a bed," said Veronica.

"Yours is quite big enough for two, I do not have the staff to move furniture just for your benefit."

Veronica blinked and said without any conviction or intention. "I must protest."

Mrs Jenkins shook her head. "I really cannot spare anyone."

She returned to the ledgers on her desk and a pile of receipts.

"Very well," said Veronica, finding it very hard to suppress the exultation she felt in her breast. She had been given permission to sleep in the same bed as Polly. Ha!

However, she settled herself. "There is another matter."

The housekeeper looked up. "What?"

"My parents' belongings."

"Yes?"

"I assume they are to be put into storage?"

"Yes, of course."

"I understand that you are overworked and have insufficient staff to cope with all this disarray," said Veronica. "But I think it inappropriate for ordinary staff to handle their clothes and what-not."

Mrs Jenkins looked suspicious.

"I believe you should do it."

The woman's face looked like a cloudy day, threatening storms. "I do not have time for that, Miss Clifford-Hughes. Do not bother me with this."

"I must insist," said Veronica firmly.

"I beg your pardon?"

"I must insist that you do it, Mrs Jenkins. There is no one else that can be trusted to be discreet about such things as the enema case, for example."

"And I can assure you, miss, that it is entirely out of the question. I do not have time."

"Then I suppose I shall have to do it," said Veronica. "If you can't."

She had to give Mrs Jenkins credit for accepting she had been outmanoeuvred with good grace. The woman smiled. "Yes, perhaps you should. It must be cleared tomorrow, I will have the trunks sent up in the morning and I will open the door at ten. You will have five hours."

On the other hand, perhaps it was Veronica who had been manipulated. She wasn't sure any more.

But at least she would be able to do what she wanted.

⸺◉⸺

"I BELIEVE I SHALL RETIRE," said Veronica at about nine in the evening. The sun had gone down not long before and its light still filled the sky. But the garden was composed of shadow.

The workmen had gone from the house and its surrounds but she could hear their noise in the distance in their camp through the open windows. Sobriety was a requirement among the workmen but she wondered how well that rule was enforced.

"I have checked the calendar," said Polly as she undid the ties of Veronica's dress. "It might be best if you were to wear a pad tonight."

Veronica was aware of it. It was part of what he driven her to be so bold with Mrs Jenkins that day, as well as being one of the reasons why she had not told Polly she would be staying the night. A sublimated desire to hurt dressed up with a justification to surprise.

"Yes, all right."

Presently she was naked. They had not lit any candles and only the dying twilight illuminated the room. Polly knelt in front of her so Veronica could step into the pad's leg holes.

"You shouldn't have to make these," said Veronica. "We can buy them mail order."

"When you have some money."

"Not long, my husband will give me an allowance. After all he will not be interested in his wife's private details."

"He might be."

Veronica remembered Edwin very clearly, his detachment and disinterest. "I doubt it."

"Do you want your nightgown?"

Veronica shook her head and sat on the bed, letting Polly arrange the pillows to support her back.

"Candle?"

"No, I don't think I ever want to light my life with candles again. I shall wait until we have the electric."

Polly bustled around tidying up ready for the morning then headed for the door. "I'll say goodnight then."

"No kiss?"

Polly turned, her fist resting on the handle. "You're in a funny mood. You always get like this before your period. I feel like you're going to bite my head off."

"Bolt the door."

"I don't think so. I should be getting back to my room."

"To Ursula?" It came out harsher than Veronica intended. Polly was right, she became quite unpleasant at this time of the month. "Sorry, I didn't mean..."

"Yes, you did."

"There's something I have to tell you," said Veronica quickly before Polly decided to leave.

"What?"

"You can stay the night." Veronica wished she was not lying in bed. Polly was too far away and it was as if they were shouting across a river that neither of them could cross.

"I can't."

"Mrs Jenkins said it was all right."

"You discussed me spending the night with Mrs Jenkins?"

Veronica felt like crying, this wasn't going the way she meant it to go, how she had imagined it would.

"No. Yes. It wasn't like that."

"You're not making any sense, Nika. We'll discuss this in the morning." She turned the handle and pulled open the door.

"No! Stop, please. Polly, please, listen. I'm not saying this very well." And now she really was crying with her tears tracking down her cheeks like raindrops on a window pane. "Please, don't go."

Polly hesitated then pushed the door closed again. She slid the lower bolt into place, fetched a chair and placed it by the bed on the opposite side to where Veronica lay.

Veronica sniffed and wiped her eyes on the sheet. She pulled it up and to hide her breasts. Not because she was ashamed but because she was trying not to lure Polly into bed with her body.

"Tell me what happened with Mrs Jenkins."

With her voice breaking, and somewhat incoherent, Veronica explained the talk she had with Mrs Jenkins. In her head, when she had rehearsed it, they had both been laughing at how clever Veronica had been and at the housekeeper's insistence they occupy the same bed.

Polly did not laugh. And Veronica cried again.

"You should have told me," said Polly.

"I wanted it to be a surprise. I thought you'd be happy."

"And Ursula?"

"I don't *know* Ursula!" said Veronica. "She's just a name. She's just the person you go to every night, who makes you feel good the way I do but asks nothing in return. Do you love her more than me?"

She burst into tears again and hated herself for being no better than a romantic heroine in a silly story.

"I do love Ursula," said Polly.

Veronica felt as if her heart had been ripped from her body, she went numb. Every dream she had shrivelled and turned to dust. She was alone, after all. She stopped trying to hold her head up and her tears fell on breasts and on the sheets.

"She's like a sister to me," said Polly. "She was there after your father raped me. I hope you never understand what it's like to have that done to you, Nika. I was broken and I believe I might have taken my own life because of my fear that he might do it again. It was Ursula who comforted me."

Veronica did not look up but she nodded. "You should go to her."

"But I don't love her the way I love you, Nika."

Veronica shook her head. "It's just the games we play. This is lust, not love. You should go to Ursula."

"I love the way you make me feel when we play our games, Nika. But I believe I truly love you."

Veronica realised her voice was no longer coming from across the bed but was beside her. She could not see clearly because her eyes stung with the tears. The bed moved and the sheets pressed into her legs. Polly's hand took hold of her chin and lifted slightly. A kerchief wiped her eyes and her cheeks.

"I could be parted from Ursula," said Polly. "But I will never be parted from you."

"Even though I want to fuck Seth and make him come, or that I will have a husband who will make me pregnant?"

"I am not you, Nika, and there are things you may do and places you may go that I cannot be with you—your husband's bed—but these things you want to do, and the ones you must do, they do not make me love you less. Even if I do not understand why you want them."

"What if my husband would like you to join us in bed?"

Polly laughed. "In that case I would gladly join you."

"And Seth?"

"I am sure Seth would be very happy to plant his seed in me as much as you. And if you desired me to let him, then I would do that for you."

"Only in my name?"

Polly smiled again and kissed her on the nose. "We shall see."

She stood up again and put her hands on her hips. She was just a shadow now the twilight had faded.

"I suppose," she said. "If Mrs Jenkins insists I sleep in the bed with you, I had better do as I am commanded."

Veronica watched the shadow become naked and felt the warm flesh touch hers.

And she was happy. For now.

⸻ ◉ ⸻

Would you like to read more about Veronica's Life?

Get your copy of **THE TASTE OF VERONICA** (ebook, paperback or hardback) from: http://taupress.com/veronica-2[1]

---

1. http://taupress.com/veronica-2?__src=BK-VL1

About the Author

The author of this book lives in a part of England that has big hills, some of which are right outside the door.

Other members of the household, apart from the humans, include an incredibly needy Russian Blue cat and a hyper-active Rhodesian Ridgeback dog. The dog likes the cat, but the cat does not like the dog. It seems the cat fails to realise his neediness could be satisfied by the dog if only he would allow it. The rest of the menagerie consists of even less pleasing creatures including lizards and snails. Very big snails. There are also children, who refuse to leave home despite having been old enough to do so for some time.

Despite all these burdens, or perhaps because of them, the author escapes into other worlds and returns with stories.